THE INGENIOUS

Mr. Peale

THE INGENIOUS

Mr. Peale

PAINTER, PATRIOT AND
MAN OF SCIENCE

Janet Wilson

Illustrated with Paintings by Charles Willson Peale

ATHENEUM BOOKS FOR YOUNG READERS

The American Philosophical Society in Philadelphia, so important to Charles Willson Peale during his lifetime, has become an invaluable source of information about him. Among its manuscript holdings is Peale's autobiography, from which I have quoted in this book. I would like to express my gratitude to the Society for enabling me to round out the story of Mr. Peale in his own words.

Atheneum Books for Young Readers
An imprint of Simon & Schuster Children's Publishing Division
1230 Avenue of the Americas
New York, New York 10020

Book design by Jessica Shatan
The text of this book is set in M Baskerville.

Printed in the United States of America
First Edition

10 9 8 7 6 5 4 3 2 1

Library of Congress Cataloging-in-Publication Data
Wilson, Janet.
The ingenious Mr. Peale: painter, patriot and man of science / by Janet Wilson ; illustrated with paintings by Charles Willson Peale.
p.   cm.
Includes bibliographical references and index.
Summary: Narrates the life of the early American portrait painter who established the first public picture gallery in America and who pursued numerous other interests including natural history.
ISBN 0-689-31884-7
1. Peale, Charles Willson, 1741–1827—Juvenile literature. 2. Painters—United States—Biography—Juvenile literature. [1. Peale, Charles Willson, 1741–1827. 2. Artists.] I. Peale, Charles Willson, 1741–1827. II. Title.
ND237.P27W55   1996
759.13—dc20
[B]   95-30818

FOR LIAM WILSON

Benjamin West, *Portrait of Charles Willson Peale*, 1767.

Courtesy of The New-York Historical Society.

CHAPTER
1

THE FIRST MEMBER OF THE PEALE FAMILY TO SET FOOT on American soil was not exactly overjoyed to be in the New World. On the other hand, Charles Peale—father of Charles Willson Peale—knew he was lucky to be alive. Back in England, he had narrowly missed being sent to the gallows at Newgate Prison.

It was a sorry turn of events for a young gentleman with a good education, from a long line of clergymen in Rutlandshire, who had prospects of an inheritance from his rich uncle. Charles Peale had a taste for fine clothes and an extravagant lifestyle that he could ill afford. This led him to embezzle a large sum of money from the London General Post Office, where he was employed after leaving Cambridge University. When his crime was discovered, he was sentenced to death in 1735. At the last minute, his sentence was commuted, and he was banished to the American colonies.

With little money in his pockets when his ship docked in

Virginia, Charles Peale began looking for work. Qualified teachers were in short supply. With his good manners and fine appearance he soon obtained a position at King William's School in Annapolis, Maryland. No mention was made, of course, of his checkered past. Nor did he disclose that his stay at Cambridge University had been brief before leaving for the high life of London.

It was not long before Charles met and married Margaret Triggs Matthews, who also never learned of his troubles with the law. Their first child was born on April 15, 1741, and named Charles Willson Peale in honor of his rich great-uncle in England.

When Charles was two years old, his father was appointed headmaster of Kent County School in Chestertown, Maryland. Having established a reputation as a good teacher, he could look forward to better days. And never far from his thoughts was the inheritance that he hoped would one day come his way. In the meantime, the family lived comfortably, if not lavishly, in quarters provided for the headmaster. In rapid succession, the Peales became the parents of two more sons and two daughters. The children were looked after by a young woman named Peggy Durgan. For the next fifty years she would remain a part of Charles Willson Peale's family.

Young Charles attended his father's school. Through the older Peale's efforts it became an institution with an excellent reputation where, as advertised in the *Maryland Gazette*, young gentlemen were taught "the Greek and Latin Tongues, Writing, Arithmetic, Merchants Accounts, Surveying, Navigation," and other subjects. Charles was a good student in Latin and mathematics, but nothing gave him more pleasure than his drawing lessons. The boy's artistic ability was soon evident, and he set about making copies of engravings of paintings by European old masters and also doing original drawings.

As the oldest child, Charles was most keenly aware of the family's limited funds. A headmaster's salary was small, and his workload was heavy. To help support his family, the elder Peale took in boarding students and did outside work such as surveying for landowners in the area. Charles often went along to help him. Efforts were also made by his father to find a better-paying job as sheriff of the county, but these were unsuccessful. All the worries, hard work, and disappointments were finally too much for Charles Peale, who suffered from gout as well. His health declined, and in 1750 he died at the age of forty-one. Although the legacy he had dreamed of never became his, he did succeed, at the end, in reclaiming his good name.

Unfortunately, that was about all he was able to leave to his family. His death left them destitute and on the brink of being homeless. The school's living quarters were needed for the new headmaster. In those days, people in such circumstances had no alternative but to turn to their relatives for help. There were no other members of the Peale family in America, however, nor did Mrs. Peale have any relatives who could come to their aid.

Had it not been for John Beale Bordley, a wealthy young plantation owner and lawyer in Maryland, the Peales would have faced a grim future. Bordley had been a shy and socially awkward student at the Kent County School and he had never forgotten the headmaster who had helped him to gain self-confidence. His gratitude for Peale's kindness to him was now expressed by making it possible for Mrs. Peale and her young children to move into a small house in Annapolis. Bordley would continue to play an important role in the life of Charles Willson Peale, and over the years he became one of his most cherished friends.

A roof over their heads met the family's most pressing need, but

Mrs. Peale had to find a way to support her brood as soon as possible. Enterprising and possessed of a cheerful disposition—qualities her son inherited—she turned to needlework and dressmaking. Like most women in colonial times, she had been taught these skills in girlhood. They could be put to good use in Annapolis, the capital of Maryland, which was an important center of social life for Maryland plantation owners and their families as well as a thriving port. There was no shortage of fashionably dressed ladies eager to add to their wardrobes.

Mrs. Peale soon had enough customers to keep her busy. Charles continued his studies, but they did not match the classical education he had received at his father's school. Mrs. Peale could not afford tuition at Annapolis's better institutions, so he had to settle for a school that provided only the basics, such as arithmetic and writing.

In his spare time, Charles enjoyed wandering abut Annapolis, taking in the sights of the town and paying close attention to the gentry in their fine clothes and carriages. These powers of observation came in handy when he returned home and made sketches for his mother of the ladies dressed in the latest styles. Charles's eye for color and design also led him to create embroidery patterns for the dresses his mother was making.

With his thirteenth birthday approaching, the time had come to make a decision about the boy's future occupation. Unlike her late husband, Mrs. Peale entertained little hope that the inheritance from England would ever become a reality for her oldest son. Given the family's limited income, further education was out of the question. One of the few paths available to a poor boy was to learn a trade by serving an apprenticeship to a craftsman. During a period of usually seven years he would be given free room and board and be trained by the master while performing a variety of chores.

It was not the life Mrs. Peale had dreamed of for Charles. It would certainly have saddened his father, who had been an educated gentleman even if he never had made much money. After discussing the merits of various trades, Charles and his mother decided that a good living could always be made as a saddler. Since horses and carriages were the principal means of transportation, people would always have a need for harnesses and saddles. Thus, in 1754, Charles Willson Peale left his childhood behind and signed on as an apprentice to Nathan Waters, Saddler, in Annapolis.

2

THE LIFE OF AN APPRENTICE IN EIGHTEENTH-CENTURY America was mostly hard work, with very little time for recreation. Charles soon discovered that the saddlery was not a very pleasant place in which to spend most of one's waking hours. The terrible smell, for one thing, was hard to get used to. The hides came directly from the tannery and had to be soaked for several weeks before they could be worked on. The job of preparing the hides was dirty and tedious. First, the hide had to be scraped with a sharp knife until it had the proper thickness. Then oil was applied to make the leather soft and pliant. All these grubby tasks fell to Charles as a beginning apprentice.

Despite the hard work, Charles took an interest in learning the many different skills that a master saddler needed in his craft. Some ability at wood carving was required in order to form the base of the saddle. The leather had to be carefully cut and shaped to fit over this base. It was also important to acquire some knowledge of metalworking. Charles was so serious and industrious as he went about learning these things that his fellow apprentices gave him the nickname of "Sobersides."

Although these fun-loving lads probably thought that Charles was a bit of a stick-in-the-mud, his master, Nathan Waters, was impressed by his hard work. As Charles's competence grew, Waters decided that his star apprentice merited some privileges. He offered to pay Charles for doing some extra work in his spare time. The boy eagerly accepted the offer, and by working in the early morning and at night after his regular chores were done, he managed to save some money. The first thing he bought was a pocket watch, but his pride in this possession soon turned to dismay when it stopped working. He was even more annoyed at being charged five shillings to have the watch repaired, only to have it stop ticking again. He was not about to hand over any more of his hard-earned money and decided to fix it himself.

Undeterred by his lack of know-how, Charles proceeded to take the watch apart. Putting all the bits and pieces back together again, however, proved to be more difficult. A few helpful hints from a local watchmaker enabled him to solve the puzzle, although the watch never became a reliable timepiece. Nonetheless it provided the opportunity to expand his range of skills.

When Charles was seventeen, he was finally able to buy a horse. Just as today's teenagers long for a car to widen their social horizons, this purchase gave him a measure of independence and the freedom to roam beyond Annapolis. One Sunday afternoon he set off to visit a young man named John Brewer, whom he had met in Annapolis. The Brewer family lived on a plantation just beyond the South River, an inlet of Chesapeake Bay. It didn't take long for

Charles to realize that, for him, the main attraction at the Brewer household was John's younger sister, fourteen-year-old Rachel. In old age when Charles Willson Peale wrote his autobiography, he lovingly described the young lady who had caught his eye:

> Miss Rachel belonged to the class of small women of fair complexion, although her hair was a dark brown colour which hung in curling ringlets over her beautiful white neck. Her face was a perfect oval; she had sprightly dark eyes; her nose straight with some few angles such as painters are fond to imitate; her mouth small and most pleasantly formed. In short, she would be called handsome amongst the most beautiful of an assembly of her sex.

After their first meeting, Charles made many return visits to the Brewer home. He soon became certain that Rachel was the girl he wanted to marry, although he realized that a wedding was far in the future. First of all, he was not allowed to marry under the terms of his apprenticeship, and he still had three years to serve. Then there was the fact that Rachel was much too young.

Marriage would have to be put on hold, but there was no reason why he couldn't court Rachel and declare his intentions in the meantime. First, however, the custom of that era decreed that he must get permission from Rachel's widowed mother. He was encouraged to believe that Rachel was fond of him; at least she didn't discourage his frequent visits. Although not exactly handsome, he was a slender young man with lively deep blue eyes, who was well mannered and took care to have a good appearance. He must have seemed like promising son-in-law material to Mrs. Brewer, who gave her consent.

Rachel was the last to get the news. She was sitting in the garden with her sister when Charles rushed out to pop the question. Not waiting until they were alone, or even first saying a few romantic words, he asked her to marry him. Rachel, stunned by his direct approach and perhaps embarrassed by her sister's presence, was tongue-tied. When she failed to reply, Charles repeated the question more insistently. She remained silent.

The young man was crushed. He was convinced that he had misread Rachel's feelings for him, but he was determined to get an answer one way or the other. His usual good manners deserted him in the heat of his anxiety. He told Rachel that he would give her one hour to make up her mind. Out of his pocket came his watch to mark the time.

Charles Willson Peale summoned up the memory of that day in his autobiography (which he wrote in the third person): "The Lady's resentment prevented any reply. The time expired. He went immediately into the House and thanked her mother for the kind entertainment he had received, and said he hoped Miss Rachel would get a better husband than he could make. That he must now take leave of the family forever."

It was not to be. Some weeks later, while out walking in Annapolis, he ran into Rachel in front of her aunt's house and begged her forgiveness for his rude behavior. She accepted his apology and agreed that he could visit her the following Sunday. On this occasion, when they were alone together in the garden, he managed to come up with a more pleasing way to ask for her hand in marriage. And this time Rachel did not hesitate to accept his proposal. They were now officially engaged.

In his autobiography, Peale recalled: "He was not more than 18 yrs. old at this time & he ever after spent all the time he could be spared from his masters service, in his attendance on the Lady, let it hail, rain or blow, no weather deterred him from crossing South river & a Creek every week to visit Miss Rachel Brewer."

Charles continued his labors in the saddlery, every day growing more eager to be on his own. Finally, at the end of December 1761, he completed his apprenticeship. He was now a qualified craftsman.

"How great the joy! how supreme the delight of freedom!" he later wrote.

> It is like water to the thirsty, like food to the hungry, or like rest to the wearyed Traveller. . . . Perhaps it is not possible for those who have never been in such a situation to fully feel the sweet, the delightfull sensations attending a release from a labour from sunrise to sunset . . . under the controls of a Master, and confined to the same walls and the same dull repetitions of the same dull labours.

CHAPTER

3

CHARLES WASTED NO TIME IN MAKING PLANS TO SET up his own saddlery in Annapolis. The first hurdle was a lack of funds for the purchase of necessary supplies, let alone for renting a shop. To his rescue came James Tilghman, an old acquaintance of his father's, who offered to lend him twenty pounds. This would enable him to go to Philadelphia to buy what he needed.

When Charles told Nathan Waters of his plans, his former master said there was no reason for him to make the trip. He could supply everything that was necessary for one hundred and fifty pounds. It might as well have been a thousand, as far as Charles was concerned, since all he had was what Tilghman loaned him. Not to worry, said Waters. He would take the twenty and allow Charles to sign a note promising to pay the rest when his business began to prosper. Charles accepted the offer and rented a shop on

Church Street near Waters's saddlery—competition that the older man was not pleased about.

Charles soon learned that he had made a poor business deal. The one hundred and fifty pounds had bought him an inadequate assortment of supplies for a new saddlery. But by this time he had signed the note and couldn't back out of the legal agreement.

A contract with a far happier outcome was signed on January 12, 1762, when Charles married Rachel Brewer, then seventeen. Since the young couple could not afford a home of their own, they moved in with Mrs. Peale and other members of the family. Less than a fortnight after the wedding, on January 21, an announcement in the *Maryland Gazette* advertised the opening of the shop of Charles Willson Peale, Saddler, who promised to perform all work "in the best, neatest and cheapest Manner."

Out of the blue, just as the saddlery was opening, Charles received a letter from England that brought astonishing news. Signed by a Captain James Digby, who said he was a cousin, the letter rekindled hopes for the inheritance so long dreamed of by Charles's father. Digby advised Charles to come at once to England to claim the estate in Oxfordshire of his great-uncle, which he said was worth two thousand pounds.

The news sent a shiver of excitement through the Peale household, but there was no money to pay for a trip to England. On the advice of a friend, Charles decided that the wisest course of action would be to contact a lawyer in England first, setting forth proof of his claim to the estate. He also sent his thanks to Captain Digby. There was no reply to either letter.

Great expectations did not pay the bills. Charles's immediate concern was to make his business a success. Thanks to friends, and especially Rachel's relatives, some orders began to come in.

Charles's brother James, who had also learned saddlemaking, worked alongside him. Throughout their lives, the two brothers would maintain a close relationship.

Charles soon realized that he could earn a better living by expanding his business to include harness making and upholstering. And before long he had acquired enough skill in metalworking to make the brass fittings for his saddles. This led him to silver-smithing and the production of simple items such as shoe buckles, bridles, and rings. For the most part, he had to make his own tools for these projects and then teach himself how to use them.

He also decided to take in a chaise-maker as a partner because of the popularity of that type of two-wheeled carriage. Prospects looked good in April 1762 when Charles celebrated his twenty-first birthday. He now had his own business and, if fortune continued to smile on him, a legacy from England. He was also now old enough to be legally responsible for his own debts, and Nathan Waters was well aware of the fact. He demanded immediate payment of interest on the note Charles had signed.

The easy terms Waters had originally proposed had led Charles to believe that his former master expected no payment of interest on the loan. With the new saddlery now taking away business from Waters, he was less inclined to wait for his money, or to show any good will toward his young competitor. Charles dug deep into his pockets and made the payment.

When the supplies bought from Waters began to run low, Charles had to travel to Norfolk to buy more leather. This would prove to be one of the most important journeys he ever made, changing the direction of his life in ways he could not yet dream of. While in Norfolk he had the opportunity to visit the home of a man who had painted several landscapes and a portrait. Like most people in colonial America, Charles had never seen real oil paintings. There were no museums or art academies then, and few professional painters. Nonetheless, he took one look at these paintings and knew they were dreadful. "Had they been better," he later wrote in his autobiography, "perhaps they would not have lead Peale to the Idea of attempting any thing in that way, but rather have smothered this faint spark of Genius."

Despite their poor quality, the paintings rekindled the interest in art Charles had shown as a young boy. As soon as he returned to Annapolis, he obtained paint and brushes from the chaise-maker and set to work making portraits of Rachel and his brother James, as well as one of himself. Those who saw his work were full of praise. Word of his artistic ability got round to a Captain Maybury, who commissioned Charles to paint portraits of him and his wife for the sum of ten pounds.

It was enough to make Charles decide, as his autobiography states, "that he possibly might do better by painting than his other Trades, and he accordingly began the sign painting business." Not everyone wanted or could afford to have a portrait painted, but many places, such as inns, shops, and other businesses, needed signs. In an era when many people never learned to read, the pictures on signs helped to identify what was being sold. A painter could also find work decorating carriages and other vehicles.

Coach paints served his purpose for these jobs, but the heavy oils were unsuitable for painting portraits. The art supplies he needed were unavailable in a small town like Annapolis. For those he would have to go to Philadelphia, the most important city in the colonies. James Tilghman was then living in Philadelphia and put Charles in touch with a local artist who had studied painting in Italy. At his studio Charles saw a palette and easel for the first time. He had been making do with his own versions of this basic art equipment, just as he had usually made his own tools for his other trades.

The art of painting was still pretty much a mystery to him. He had no idea how to grind pigment, mix, or apply paints. Indeed, he knew the names of only the most common colors. This was a great disadvantage when he finally located Christopher Marshall's color shop on Chestnut Street in Philadelphia. Rather than reveal his ignorance about how to place an order, Charles entered the shop and asked for a list of available colors, including prices. He would return to make his purchases, he told Marshall, after looking over the list and deciding what he could afford.

His next stop was Rivington's bookstore, where he purchased a two-volume edition of *The Handmaid to the Arts*. Published in London in 1752, these books provided the basic instructions for creating all types of art. For the next few days, Charles did nothing but study them. So intent was he on mastering every detail that he barely took time to eat or sleep. Finally finished, he returned with new confidence to the color shop and bought what he needed.

Back home in Annapolis, Charles realized that the books were helpful but couldn't supply all the technical information about painting that he needed. As there were no art schools, his only hope was to get some training by watching an artist at work. Among the handful of portrait painters in Maryland at that time was John Hesselius, who lived near Annapolis. Charles had no extra money for art lessons, but he had something just as valuable. He offered Hesselius "one of the best saddles with its complete furniture, for permission to see him paint a picture."

Hesselius accepted the offer and allowed Charles to observe him painting two portraits. Every step was keenly watched. For the first time, Charles saw how a canvas was stretched on a wood frame and then sized to provide a nonabsorbent surface for the paint. He noted how Hesselius constructed the figures and paid special attention to their costumes and other decorative details. When the two paintings were completed, Hesselius offered a bonus. He invited Charles to join him in working on a portrait; he would paint half of the face, and Charles the other half. The aspiring young artist—still struggling to learn the basics of this vocation—could not yet dream that one day he would be a far greater painter than his first instructor.

CHAPTER

·————————·

4

THE FUTURE, WHICH HAD SEEMED SO BRIGHT, SOON MET
the darker reality of the present. The Peales' first child, a
baby girl, was born in the spring of 1763 but lived only twelve
days. That personal sorrow was followed by a series of financial
troubles. Peale's partner, the chaise-maker, who owed him a
large sum of money, ran off with all the shop's funds. The next
blow, in October 1763, was Nathan Waters's demand for full
payment of his loan, as he was planning to move away from
Annapolis.

With other creditors at his door as well, Peale had to raise some
cash immediately. He sold off the saddles and other merchandise in
his shop at bargain prices, and as a result made little profit. This
also depleted his stock so severely that it would take time to make
enough new items to generate income. When an acquaintance
asked him to repair a large number of defective watches he had

———————

imported, Peale seized upon a new way out of his troubles. He would turn this self-taught skill into a business.

On February 23, 1764, he placed an announcement in the *Maryland Gazette* advertising his services. One thing he failed to consider was the angry reaction of a local watchmaker, William Knapp, who promptly warned the public against the "unskillful and injudicious practice of some Men, who assumed the knowledge of a Business to which they were only pretenders." Knapp then cited his own training in London and Dublin with the "most eminent" watchmakers. It was enough of a blow to convince Peale that this had not been a good idea.

Down but not out, he took to the road with a two-wheeled cart loaded with saddles and harnesses, tools for mending clocks and watches, and other supplies. Perhaps people living in the rural Maryland counties would welcome his services at their doorsteps. There was some demand, but Peale quickly found that getting paid was another matter. The country folk were used to obtaining their saddles and other needs on credit at local stores and then paying their debts at harvest time when the crops were sold. Peale, who needed more than promises of future payment, headed back to Annapolis.

If he had met with more success in business, it's possible that Peale might have been content to remain a tradesman who painted only as a hobby in his spare time. But as one venture after another failed to bring financial security, he began to give more thought to making a living as an artist.

In the summer of 1764, however, there were other matters claiming his attention. They unleashed a chain of events that would play a major role in propelling him toward a career in art. In the proprietary colony of Maryland, which was land given outright to Lord Baltimore, of the Calvert family, a bitter political battle had developed between the "court" and "country" parties. The court party represented the interests of the colony's original owners, or proprietors, whose influence was so great that all public positions were held by their friends and supporters. Their candidate for a seat in the provincial assembly was Dr. George Steuart, the mayor of Annapolis. His opponent, backed by the country party, was Samuel Chase, a fiery young lawyer determined to break the court party's stranglehold on the reins of power. Most importantly, Chase had won the support of Charles Carroll, Barrister (as he was known to distinguish him from several prominent men with the same name). Also campaigning actively for Chase were the Sons of Freedom, who gained a new member, Charles Willson Peale, in the summer of 1764.

The court party had the backing of many influential citizens in Annapolis. Unfortunately, some of them were people to whom Peale owed money. It did not go unnoticed that the young saddler was parading around town with the Sons of Freedom. And it was known that he had painted many of the banners they carried, which expressed views that Peale's creditors strongly disagreed with. Words of warning were sent to Peale. If he wanted to avoid being arrested for not paying his debts, he would be wise to stop campaigning for Chase or associating with the Sons of Freedom.

Despite these threats, Peale refused to give up a cause he believed in, but he was well aware of the risk he was taking. His one hope of being rescued from debt was the legacy supposedly waiting for him in England. With that two thousand pounds, his problems would be solved. More than two years had passed since the arrival of Captain Digby's letter, and no further word had been received. He turned for help to Charles Carroll, Barrister. On

Peale's behalf, he wrote to his attorney in London and sent the legal documents supporting the young man's claim to the inheritance.

In the meantime, Peale had landed in enough trouble to make it unwise to wait around in Annapolis for a letter from England. (In those days it could often take months.) That November Samuel Chase won the election—the first time in the history of Annapolis that the court party had been defeated. The party's angry supporters, seeing their power in the assembly weakened, sought revenge on those who had actively backed Chase. Four of Peale's creditors had writs for debt served on him. Either he must pay immediately all that he owed them, or he would be arrested and sent to debtors' prison. Since it turned out that he owed nine hundred pounds but had assets of only three hundred pounds, his options were limited. He decided that his best move was to get out of town right away and not return until he had earned enough money to settle his debts.

On a spring evening in 1765 Peale and his wife secretly left Annapolis. There was barely enough time to pack a few belongings, which were taken out of the house in shifts to avoid tipping off the neighbors that they were going away. Brother James carried Peale's painting supplies down to the wharf; a little later his other brother, St. George, came along with a bundle of clothing. Soon they were aboard a ferry that carried them across Chesapeake Bay to Queen Anne's County. There the young couple found refuge with Charles's sister Margaret Jane, who was married to James M'Mordie, who operated an inn at Tuckahoe Bridge.

There was plenty of room for them, and even the prospect of some work for Peale. One of their neighbors, a Captain Cole, had earlier seen some of his paintings and expressed an interest in having some portraits done of his family. Peale set to work at once.

The captain was delighted with the results, raising the artist's hopes that others would offer him commissions.

He had found safety in Queen Anne's County, but not for long. One of the area's residents was James Tilghman, who had been kind enough several years earlier to lend him twenty pounds for his saddlery. He was now feeling less charitable toward Peale, who had neglected to keep in touch with him about paying back the loan, or even paying interest on it. To make matters worse, Tilghman was a strong supporter of the court party and had been furious with Peale for backing Samuel Chase.

When he learned that Peale was in the area, he had a writ issued for his arrest because of nonpayment of the debt. Luckily for Peale, word reached him through a friend of what was about to happen. With only a few hours to hatch a new escape plan, he purchased a horse and packed up a small bundle of clothes and his painting supplies.

This time his destination was the home of another sister, Elizabeth, who lived in Virginia. Once across the Maryland border, he would be beyond the reach of its authorities. This trip, however, would be made alone. Rachel was pregnant and not up to such a tiring overland journey. Sorrowfully he said goodbye to her and set out on the difficult six-day trip. Little did he realize that it would be over a year before he would see her again.

CHAPTER

5

SISTER ELIZABETH'S HOME IN VIRGINIA PROVIDED A SAFE haven for Peale, but he had no sooner arrived than he was on the move again. Elizabeth's husband, Robert Polk, owned a small schooner and was preparing to sail north with a cargo of corn. Peale eagerly accepted the offer to join him on the voyage. It would put even greater distance between himself and his creditors and also give him the opportunity to look around New England.

After a seven-day trip, they arrived in Boston on July 14, 1765. The next morning, while Polk attended to business, Peale set off to find a store that sold art supplies. At the color shop of John Moffatt he found what he was looking for—and much more. After taking Peale's order, Moffatt invited him to look at some paintings that had been done by his late uncle, John Smibert. He promised the young man that he was in for a treat and led the way upstairs to what had once been Smibert's studio.

The paintings hanging on the wall more than lived up to Moffatt's words. In addition to copies of paintings by the Italian old masters, there were some unfinished portraits and sketches of classical subjects. Peale was dazzled by the quality of the work, which was so much better than that of Hesselius or any other artist he had yet encountered. He had never heard of Smibert but learned from Moffatt that the Scottish-born artist, who died in 1751, had earned a reputation in New England for his portraits. The copies of Italian paintings had been done during his earlier travels to that country. Many of them caught Peale's eye, for as a child he had copied black-and-white engravings of them. Here, for the first time, he was able to see them in brilliant color. As he always did whenever he got a chance to look at a real oil painting, he studied the work closely. Each picture was a learning experience for him, providing lessons in composition, color, paint handling, and all the elements of a fine work of art.

Captain Polk's business in Boston turned out to be less rewarding than Peale's experience in the city. Unable to sell all his cargo there, he planned to sail to Newburyport, about forty miles north of Boston. Peale would have preferred to stay in Boston, but his limited funds left him no choice but to go along.

When they arrived in port, he set about painting the outside of the schooner. It was one way he could repay the kindness of his brother-in-law. He was eager, however, to undertake painting of a different kind after seeing Smibert's work. When he had some time, he painted a small self-portrait. Quite pleased with the work, he hung it in a cabin aboard the vessel, where it was noticed by Nathaniel Carter, a wealthy merchant who had come to discuss business with Polk. Carter promptly commissioned Peale to paint portraits of his three children.

Only one other portrait commission came his way in Newburyport, but Peale soon found plenty of things to keep him busy. The patriotic fervor of his Annapolis days was rekindled in New England, which was in an uproar over the British Parliament's passage of the Stamp Act in March 1765. This despised revenue act, which was to become effective that November, would require all legal documents, licenses, newspapers, and advertisements to have a tax stamp.

Parliament had passed the law in order to raise money after the heavy costs incurred during the recent French and Indian Wars. Many colonists felt that the new tax was a shabby way to thank them for their contributions of manpower and supplies to help the British win victory. Nor did they like the idea of British tax agents snooping into all their business dealings. But most of all they were outraged that their voices were not being heard in Parliament. It was a clear case of taxation without representation.

They could be heard loud and clear in the colonies, however. In Newburyport, noisy demonstrations were taking place, many of them organized by the Sons of Liberty. In September 1765 Peale joined their ranks and was soon enlisted to paint banners for their marches. Crowds of angry citizens gathered, and on a tree in the center of town they hung an effigy of Andrew Oliver, the local stamp distributor. It was later set afire, and as the fragments fell to the ground, people stamped their boots on them and shouted, "Stamp him! Stamp him!"

With prospects for earning money in Newburyport looking bleak, Peale decided to return to Boston in the hope that the larger city would offer more chances of work. Luck was with him when he arrived, for he found an innkeeper willing to provide board for only two dollars a week if Peale would give drawing lessons to his son.

Peale then called on John Moffatt, hoping that the owner of the color shop might be able to help him line up some portrait commissions. Moffatt said he would be glad to do what he could, but informed Peale that he had serious competition. Anyone who was anyone in Boston wanted only John Singleton Copley to paint his or her portrait. Perhaps, suggested Moffatt, he should pay a visit to Copley, who had more offers of work than he could possibly handle.

Charles was astonished to learn that this most notable of colonial artists was only twenty-seven years old—a mere three years older than himself! His innate talent and dedicated effort, since boyhood, to master the techniques of painting had brought Copley to the peak of his profession in Boston. He had developed a distinctive style that captured the character of a subject. Facial features and all the details of the sitter's clothing—the lustrous silk of a gown or the ruffles of a gentleman's waistcoat—were rendered with great care.

If Smibert's pictures had impressed Peale, he was positively bowled over by those of Copley. As he wrote in his autobiography, "The sight of Mr. Copley's picture room was a great feast to Peale." Here was a superb artist from whom he could learn a great deal if only Copley could be persuaded to give him some instruction. To Peale's great joy, Copley allowed him to come to his studio and copy a portrait. He also offered him some lessons in painting miniatures. These small-scale pictures, he informed Peale, were very popular and could provide a good source of income.

A few commissions for miniatures came his way, thanks to Copley, and he also earned twelve dollars for painting a portrait. But his hopes again began to fade, with "his Cash wasting daily away, without any prospects of employment," as he later recalled.

It was clear that Copley's immense popularity would make it difficult for him to do well as an artist in Boston. There was a much better chance of getting commissions in the Maryland-Virginia area, Peale decided, where there were fewer artists, and none of Copley's caliber.

There was an even more compelling reason to return home. He had received word that Rachel had given birth to a boy. Longing to see her and the baby, he located a ship bound for Virginia and managed to obtain free passage from the captain.

Still unsolved was the problem of his debts back in Annapolis. Rachel might be waiting for him with open arms, but his creditors would also be there, waving writs ordering him to prison. He must find a way to earn some money before setting foot in the town. When the ship docked in Virginia in the spring of 1766, opportunity knocked. James Arbuckle, a wealthy young plantation owner, came aboard the ship and entered the cabin where Peale's self-portrait was hanging. It was the very same painting that had won him favor in Newburyport, and once again it charmed a viewer. Arbuckle asked to meet the artist and took an instant liking to him. He invited Peale to visit at his plantation and paint portraits of himself, his wife, and children.

For the next six months, Peale lived in comfort with the Arbuckle family in Accomac, Virginia. The two men became good friends, sharing in particular an interest in all things mechanical. Peale taught his host all about clock and watch repairing, which remained a hobby for the rest of Arbuckle's life. His wife was delighted to have such a lively house guest who could not only paint her portrait but also join in an evening of singing and music making.

Peale obtained other portrait commissions, as friends and neigh-

The Edward Lloyd Family, 1771.

Courtesy, Winterthur Museum.

bors of the Arbuckles learned of his artistic ability. There was also time to work on mastering all that he had learned from Copley. The stiff figures in Peale's earlier work were replaced by subjects posed in the more natural, relaxed manner he had seen in Copley's portraits. This pleasant interlude, away from the daily struggle to make ends meet, enabled Peale to take a great leap forward in the quality of his painting.

But the time had come to leave. He could no longer bear being separated from his wife and family. Arbuckle tried to tempt him to stay by offering to give Peale a piece of land nearby and build him a house for his family. "But this was no way for Peale to get forward in the world," he later wrote. The events of the past year had altered the direction of his life. Away from the saddlery, lacking the tools of his various trades, he had been all but forced to support himself by painting and to "make every effort to excell in that art." It was the road he was now determined to follow. Looking back, Peale would regard his financial troubles and exile as a blessing, for without them he "might have been content to drudge in an unnoticed manner through life."

He had earned some money during the past six months, but not enough to settle his debts. Again, one of his paintings came to the rescue. It was a recent work based on a portrait by the famous English artist Sir Joshua Reynolds. Proud of how well it had turned out, he sent the picture to Charles Carroll, Barrister, in Annapolis. Carroll was pleased with the gift and decided it was time to arrange a way for Peale to return home without risking his freedom. He drew up a letter of license, which would allow Peale to have four more years to settle his debts. All but four of his most stubborn creditors agreed to sign the papers. Fortunately, Rachel received at this time a modest inheritance from her father's estate, which the foursome agreed to accept as security until the debts could be paid in full.

In October 1766 the Peale family had a joyful reunion in Annapolis, and the proud father got to see his baby son, James, for the first time. At last the way seemed clear for Peale to make a fresh start in his hometown.

CHAPTER

·————————·

6

THE PAINTING SENT TO CHARLES CARROLL, BARRISTER, helped pave the way for Peale's return to Annapolis. But another picture, sent to his old friend John Beale Bordley, would provide the ticket that led Peale farther away from home than he had ever gone.

The painting arrived at the home of Bordley's sister, Elizabeth Bordley, where he was staying while in Annapolis to attend a meeting of the Governor's Council. Bordley took a keen interest in art and painted as a hobby at his large plantation on Wye Island in Chesapeake Bay. Although he was eager to unwrap the picture to see what progress his young friend had made, the hour was late. His sister suggested that they wait until the next day.

What happened next was told to Peale and described in his autobiography: "When he [Bordley] rose in the morning he went into a cold room where the picture was put, before he had

John Beale Bordley, 1770.

National Gallery of Art, Washington. Gift of the Barra Foundation, Inc.

gartered up his stockings, and staid there Viewing it near 2 hours, and when he came out he said to his sister, 'Something must and shall be done for Charles.' "

Bordley had in mind nothing less than a year of art study in London, where the young man could make even greater progress as a painter. He summoned Peale and asked if he would be interested in this. It was a difficult question to answer for someone who had just been reunited with his wife and family after a year-long absence. But he knew that he could not turn down such a fabulous offer. And from a practical standpoint, it would help him to become a successful artist, ensuring the well-being of his family.

Bordley turned to an influential circle of friends and colleagues on the Governor's Council to raise money for the venture. He reckoned that they might be willing to bank on Peale in the hope that he would fulfill his artistic promise and bring honor to Maryland. Among the eleven people including himself who provided the funding were Charles Carroll, Barrister, and Governor Horatio Sharpe.

In an effort to put Peale in good hands in London, Carroll obtained a letter of introduction for him to Benjamin West. Born near Philadelphia in 1738, West was only three years older than Peale but was already a highly respected artist in London. Wealthy benefactors in Philadelphia had spotted his talent early on and enabled him to go abroad to study painting. At first West did portraits, but then turned to history painting, for which he was most renowned. So great was West's success in England that in 1772 he would be appointed History Painter to King George III. Although he settled in England and later became president of the Royal Academy, he never forgot his homeland and always gave a warm welcome to American artists.

Making a connection with West was the first priority, but

Bordley was also looking out for Peale's financial interests. He gave the young man a letter of introduction to his half-brother in London, Edmund Jenings, who might be able to help him learn the true status of his legacy. After all this time, Peale's letters to England had remained unanswered.

With a heavy heart, Peale again said goodbye to his wife, consoled only by the prospect of future artistic success and perhaps the legacy. There was one thing to cheer up this Son of Liberty as he made his departure. The British Parliament had given in to colonial protests and repealed the Stamp Act earlier that year. Thus when the *Brandon* set sail for London in December 1766, it carried Peale and many boxes of unused revenue stamps.

The trip across the Atlantic took eight weeks. They were eight miserable weeks of gales and heavy storms that left Peale almost constantly seasick. On one particularly stormy day, gigantic waves swept over the ship, flooding his cabin and completely soaking all his belongings. On February 13, 1767, the ship finally docked in London. Too weak and exhausted to celebrate his safe arrival, he crept off to an inn to get some rest.

When he was feeling better, Peale set off to buy some new clothes to replace his water-damaged garments. He didn't want to look like a shipwrecked sailor at his first meeting with Benjamin West. Like his father before him, Peale had a taste for fine clothing. He located a tailor and ordered a fashionable, light blue half-dress suit, along with a beaver hat, gloves, and black stockings.

His first meeting with West was all that he could have wished for. The artist was happy to see a fellow American and immediately showed Peale around his studio on Castle Street. Sketches, cartoons (the full-scale design for a work), and paintings not yet finished filled a series of rooms. Best of all was West's promise to take him on as a student. But first, he said, they must find nearby lodgings for the newcomer. Accompanied by West, Peale found a place to stay on Silver Street at Golden Square. With an address like that, how could he fail?

No stranger to hard work, Peale now dedicated almost all of his energies to art. Every aspect of it interested him. "For he was not contented with knowing how to paint in one way," Peale later wrote, "but he engaged in the whole circle of arts, except at painting in enamel. And also at Modeling, and casting in plaster of Paris. . . . And his application was such, that at several times he had nearly brought himself into a bad state of health. But with moderate exercise in the open air, the vigor of youth soon reinstated him."

Peale became especially interested in painting miniatures. Since West worked on a much larger, grander scale, he arranged to borrow some examples from fellow artists so that Peale might copy and learn from them. Like West's other students, Peale served as his studio assistant. This often involved painting the drapery or other minor parts of a picture West was working on. And handyman that he was, Peale proved helpful in other ways. As William Dunlap wrote in his history of the arts published in 1834, "Mr. West painted to the last with a palette which Peale had most ingeniously mended for him, after he [West] had broken it and thrown it aside as useless. It was a small palette, but he never used any other for his largest pictures."

Peale spent most of his evenings studying books on art and also began to teach himself French (the language of his grandmother). He had little time—and even less money—for the various forms of entertainment that appealed to most visitors to London. In truth, he was intensely homesick and not much interested in gadding about. As he later wrote, "Had Mrs. Peale accompanied him, he might then have enjoyed the amusements which the great city affords, but he always felt himself lonely even amidst the crowds."

One thing he did want to see while in London was the work of the great European old master painters, little of which could be found in the American colonies. As no public art museums existed in London at that time, such masterworks could only be seen by gaining access to the homes of the wealthy private collectors who owned them. West's connections made this possible, but Peale soon discovered that such excursions were expensive. In these splendid houses, tips were expected by all the servants as he went from room to room.

As a result, most of the paintings he saw were by contemporary artists such as Sir Joshua Reynolds. He was particularly impressed by the portraits painted by Angelica Kauffmann, whose studio was near his lodgings in Golden Square. He would later use her as an example to argue his belief (not widely shared) that women could excel in the arts equally with men.

Within a few months of Peale's arrival in London, Parliament passed the Townshend Acts. Revenue was to be raised in the colonies by imposing import duties on a variety of items, ranging from lead and paper to tea. Strong resistance to these taxes erupted in America, leading to the Boston Massacre in 1770 and the Boston Tea Party three years later.

Parliament's action had a more immediate response from a certain Son of Liberty on English soil. He vowed that "he would never pull off his hat as the King passed by. . . and determined he would do all in his power to render his Country independent."

CHAPTER

7

NOW THAT PEALE WAS MORE OR LESS SETTLED IN LONDON, the time had come to find out where he stood regarding his legacy. He turned for help to Bordley's half-brother, Edmund Jenings, who became a good friend and patron throughout Peale's stay in England. They were able to track down a copy of the will of his great-uncle, Dr. Charles Wilson, which indicated that Peale had a valid claim to the legacy now that the doctor's daughter and Charles Peale were both dead.

This was not the opinion of Peale's uncle in Rutlandshire, the Reverend Joseph Digby. Peale wrote to him and inquired about his son, James Digby, no doubt referring to the letter sent to him in America. The clergyman said he had no son by that name; someone must have been playing a trick on Peale.

It occurred to him that he had received the letter shortly after his apprenticeship ended. And the more he thought about it, the more he realized that the handwriting on the letter was very similar to that of Nathan Waters's clerk. Although he couldn't be sure, it was possible that the lad had heard him speak of his future prospects and had written the letter as a hoax.

Despite this revelation, Peale did not entirely lose hope until he met with his uncle in London. Digby gave him to understand that other claims to the estate might be more valid than his own. And quite likely it was at this meeting that Peale learned for the first time of his father's disgrace in England (a subject he never discussed in his autobiography).

Unfortunately, the legal documents that might have made a case for Peale's claim were gone. The lawyer to whom he had sent them had died, which was why he had never heard from him, and now the papers could not be located. Given that fact as well as his lack of funds to undertake a lawsuit in support of his claim, Peale decided to close the book forever on the legacy.

It was during this period, in 1767, that Benjamin West painted a portrait of his student. He depicted Peale with an air of nobility, his paintbrush held high like a king's scepter. In view of Peale's lost hopes, West may have meant to express his belief that the dedicated life of an artist made a person far worthier than did noble birth or inherited wealth.

At an exhibition of the Society of Artists in 1767, Peale saw a portrait of Benjamin Franklin, who was then living in London and representing the commercial interests of Pennsylvania and other colonies. Peale knew of Franklin's many accomplishments and had been keenly interested in his famous experiment with a kite in a thunderstorm, which had proved the presence of electricity in lightning.

On the spur of the moment, the young artist decided to call on

Franklin, even though he lacked the customary letter of introduction. A servant responded to his knock at the door of Franklin's residence and directed him to a room, without announcing his arrival to Franklin. Standing in the doorway, Peale caught his first glimpse of the distinguished gentleman, who did not see him since all of his attention was focused on the pretty young lady perched on his knee. Unable to resist the opportunity, Peale pulled out his notebook and made a quick sketch of the pair. Then, retracing his steps down the hall, he made a noisier approach to the room to alert Franklin.

Like the good doctor, Peale's interest in all things mechanical was unbounded. Franklin showed him some of the electrical experiments he was conducting and discussed some of his inventions. They would get together many times in the future when both men were back in America, and Franklin's support would be of great help to Peale.

By the end of the summer of 1767, Peale was longing to return home. News of the death of his two-year-old son, combined with his loneliness, made him decide to leave England in November. When Charles Carroll, Barrister, learned of this, he wrote to Peale urging him to stay on: "You are to Consider that you will never be able to make up to your self and family the Loss of the opportunity, and that those by whom you have been Assisted will be sorry to find their money Thrown away." Carroll also advised him to reconsider his inclination to specialize in painting miniatures, as he saw a far greater demand in America for larger portraits.

West also urged Peale to stay in London. Finally realizing the wisdom of their advice, and given some additional funding by his Maryland patrons, he remained in London for more than a year.

Commissions from Jenings to paint several portraits also helped with expenses.

Had he left England earlier, Peale would have missed several opportunities that helped advance his career. He became a member of the Society of Artists, and in April 1768 he exhibited four works at their spring exhibition. A far more important professional stepping-stone was a commission from Jenings to paint a monumental portrait of William Pitt, the Earl of Chatham. Pitt's eloquent voice in Parliament proposing the repeal of the Stamp Act had made him a hero in the American colonies. Jenings planned to send the portrait to Westmoreland County, Virginia, as his personal gift to the citizens there who had rallied opposition to the revenue act.

Peale had no luck getting his subject to pose, so he had to rely on a life-size statue and bust of Pitt that had recently been completed by sculptor Joseph Wilton. In Peale's portrait, the British statesman is dressed like an ancient Roman consul in toga and sandals. Defending the claims of the American colonies, Pitt holds a copy of the Magna Carta in one hand; with the other, he gestures toward a statue of British Liberty trampling underfoot a petition of the New York legislature that had been rejected by the House of Commons.

Peale also painted a smaller version of this portrait, which he later presented to the state of Maryland. And hoping for some future profit from the work, he made a large mezzotint, engraved with the words "Worthy of Liberty, Mr. Pitt scorns to invade the Liberties of other People."

The portrait was well received in Virginia, although it does not approach the quality of Peale's later work. Perhaps if Pitt had been able to pose for the artist, some of the stiffness of the figure might have been avoided. However, classical allegories and history painting, which West excelled at, were not suited to Peale's personal and artistic inclinations.

In March 1769 Peale boarded a ship bound for Maryland. Along with the many paintings he had done in London, he took home as a farewell gift from West his "throne chair." This large armchair, used when he was painting a portrait, sat on a revolving platform that could be adjusted to position the sitter in relation to the source of light.

Peale also took home art supplies that would be hard to obtain in the colonies, but he would not be wearing new clothes in the latest London fashion when he greeted his family. By this time his motto had become "Buy American" whenever possible.

CHAPTER

8

A VOYAGE LASTING TWELVE WEEKS, EVEN ON CALM SEAS, would make any traveler happy to reach port. For Peale, the joy of being home after an absence of more than two years was unbounded. How he had missed Rachel! And after living amid strangers, it was so good to see his mother and two brothers, James and St. George. As the head of the family, Peale saw no reason why they shouldn't all live together. When it came to domestic arrangements, his philosophy throughout his life was the more the merrier. Other members of the family would come and go, but ever present was his old nurse, Peggy Durgan.

"This now happy family," Peale later wrote, "lived in the utmost harmony together, so pleasing to me that I began with portraits of the whole in one piece, emblematical of family concord." The painting he was referring to, *The Peale Family Group*, is one of the masterpieces of early American art. It depicts Peale giving St.

The Peale Family Group, ca. 1772.

Courtesy of The New-York Historical Society.

George a drawing lesson, as members of the family gather around the table.

More than likely, St. George did not have such a large audience when, in fact, he did receive some lessons from his brother. As the chief clerk of the Maryland Land Office, he was much more comfortable adding up numbers than holding a drawing pencil. When Peale offered to give him lessons, St. George responded that "he did not believe he could be taught to make the likeness of a face in seven years."

This attitude did not accord with Peale's firm belief that any intelligent person could develop his or her talents. A good mind, he stated, is like rich soil, requiring only proper planting and cultivation to bear fruit. With great satisfaction, he noted that "within three months St. George . . . could paint a tolerable portrait in Crayons."

Brother James was so impressed by St. George's progress that he also took art lessons from Peale. Here was a real talent, who would later gain renown as a painter of miniatures. And when the next generation of Peales was growing up, the head of the family taught his sons and daughters to draw and paint. Over the years he succeeded in making good amateur artists of most of the family members he taught, and in several cases, notably Rembrandt and Raphaelle Peale, they became highly accomplished painters.

Earning enough money to pay off his old debts was still a thorny problem for Peale upon his return to Maryland. Happily, his efforts in London had improved his career prospects. He was a much better painter than before, and the news was getting around. His portrait of William Pitt, installed in the Westmoreland County Courthouse in Virginia, had boosted his reputation in the region. Visitors to his painting room in Annapolis could see the second version of the work. In the eyes of the well-to-do people likely to commission a portrait, a London-trained artist like Peale was preferred to the homegrown variety.

It was Edmund Jenings in London, however, who gave Peale his first important commission during this period, a portrait of his half-brother, John Beale Bordley. Peale's fondness for the subject must have made this a commission he undertook with special enthusiasm. The Maryland lawyer turned gentleman farmer, shown on his Wye Island plantation, is posed among patriotic symbols that identify him as a defender of American liberty.

Peale knew he could not depend on Annapolis alone to supply him with enough patrons. Many more commissions would come from the wealthy owners of plantation houses on the shores of the Chesapeake and its tributaries. In these portraits the subjects were gracefully posed in domestic settings that often included a view of their property. Unlike the stiff formal poses often seen in the work of other colonial artists, Peale conveyed a sense of the warmth and spirit of his subjects in these portraits known as "conversation pieces." Also much to their liking was his ability to render all the details of their fashionable clothing.

An even more promising destination for Peale was Philadelphia. As the center of commerce in the colonies, it offered unlimited opportunities for an artist with talent and good connections. Peale had both, and in the winter of 1769 he began making trips there. Jenings arranged for him to get a portrait commission from one of the city's most prominent citizens. John Dickinson was a lawyer and author of *Letters of a Pennsylvania Farmer*, in which he had denounced the Townshend Acts. Pleased with his portrait, he recommended the artist to his cousin, the wealthy merchant John Cadwalader. Peale's portrait of the Cadwalader family is one of his

The John Cadwalader Family, 1772.

Philadelphia Museum of Art: The Cadwalader Collection.

Purchased with funds contributed by the Pew Memorial Trust
and gift of an anonymous donor.

finest conversation pieces. Both patrons encouraged him to settle in Philadelphia. Peale was eager to move, but he realized he would have to bide his time until his debts were paid off in Annapolis.

Another important commission came his way in 1772, but this time Peale faced a reluctant sitter. George Washington was then a forty-year-old colonel in the Virginia militia. Only to please his wife, Martha, did he finally agree to pose for a portrait. He wears the uniform of his militia regiment in what is the only known portrait of Washington painted before the American Revolution. Their paths would cross many times in the years ahead, in both war and peace. Washington posed for Peale on seven different occasions, and from these sittings the artist painted at least sixty portraits.

The birth of a daughter in 1772 was an occasion for rejoicing in the Peale household, but it quickly turned to sorrow. Rachel contracted smallpox during an epidemic; she recovered, but baby Margaret died. Once again, the Peales were childless. The grieving mother asked her husband to paint a picture of the baby, expecting a portrait of her in the bloom of young life.

Instead he painted *Rachel Weeping*, which shows the grief-stricken mother beside the baby, who is wearing a white dress for burial. Nearby is a table with bottles of medicine that had failed to save her life. The work depicted a tragedy that was all too common in an era of limited medical knowledge. Rachel could not bring herself to look at the picture, and for many years it hung behind a curtain in Peale's painting room.

During the next few years Peale was frequently on the move, working on portrait commissions in Maryland and Virginia as well as in Philadelphia. All his efforts were focused on paying off his debts so that he could move to Philadelphia. In the four years after his return from London, he completed at least 150 paintings.

Rachel Weeping, 1772–1776.

Philadelphia Museum of Art: Given by the Barra Foundation, Inc.

In February 1774 Mrs. Peale gave birth to a son, who was named Raphaelle—the first of many sons and daughters to be named for a famous artist. In all, Peale fathered seventeen children, eleven of whom lived to adulthood.

The artist was making financial headway, but meanwhile war clouds were gathering in the American colonies. The Boston Tea Party in December 1773 had led the British Parliament to close the city's port until all the tea that had been dumped in the harbor was paid for. This and other "Intolerable Acts" of Parliament rallied the other colonies to the side of Massachusetts.

In Annapolis, among the citizens expressing their concern was William Eddis. "All America is in a flame!—I hear strange language every day," he wrote in a letter to a friend in London. "The colonists are ripe for any measures that will tend to the preservation of what they call, their natural liberty." In May 1774 a rump assembly composed of a group of members of the Virginia House of Burgesses met in an unofficial session in Williamsburg and called for a congress of the American colonies. Other colonies supported the idea. Thus early in September the Continental Congress held its first meeting in Philadelphia in order "to consult upon the present unhappy State of the Colonies."

Peale, who was spending the winter of 1774–1775 in Baltimore working on commissions, shared the outrage of his fellow colonists. He was therefore more than happy to paint a flag for the Independent Company of Baltimore. Once again, the Son of Liberty unfurled his patriotism in a banner that depicted "Liberty trampling upon Tyranny," with a motto proclaiming "Representation or no Taxation."

A winter's hard work and thrifty habits finally put Peale on the

Mrs. James Smith and Grandson, 1775.

National Museum of American Art, Smithsonian Institution.

Gift of Mr. and Mrs. Wilson Levering Smith, Jr. and Museum Purchase.

road to paying off his debts. When it came to collecting money owed to him, the artist showed less patience than his own creditors. Annoyed by the lack of prompt payment from one patron, he placed a notice in the *Maryland Gazette* in September 1774:

MR. ELIE VALETTE, PAY ME FOR
PAINTING YOUR FAMILY PICTURE.
CHARLES PEALE

Valette had this to say in the next issue:

MR. CHARLES WILSON PEALE,
ALIAS CHARLES PEALE—YES, YOU SHALL
BE PAID: BUT NOT BEFORE YOU HAVE
LEARNED TO BE LESS INSOLENT.
ELIE VALETTE

In August 1775 Peale could at last send the good news to Jenings: "I have but just now worked myself out of Debt, except my debts of gratitude." This should have been a time to celebrate, but it was marred by Peale's growing awareness that a revolution was likely to take place.

In December 1775 the artist finally made the move to Philadelphia, where he found its citizens in a frenzy of preparations for the coming war. While he searched for a house to rent, Rachel stayed with relatives in Maryland. It was there that she gave birth to a daughter, named Angelica Kauffmann in honor of the artist Peale had admired in London.

Plans had to be made for his family's arrival, but there were also old acquaintances to see, such as Benjamin Franklin, and new patrons to meet. Peale was soon involved in making his own contribution to the war effort. He had met David Rittenhouse, a famous astronomer and instrument maker, and together they experimented in the home manufacture of gunpowder and developed a rifle with telescopic sights.

In mid-June of 1776, Peale's family arrived and settled into the house he had rented on Arch Street. It was just a short walk over to the Statehouse, where on July 8 he stood and listened to the Declaration of Independence being read to the assembled citizens.

CHAPTER

9

Holding a musket instead of a paintbrush was alien to Peale's gentle, peace-loving nature. Yet his sense of patriotism and deep concern for his family led him to enlist in the Philadelphia Associators, a volunteer militia organized to defend the city. In a diary entry for August 9, 1776, he wrote: "Entered as a common soldier in Captain Peters's company of militia. Went on guard that night." By November he had been promoted to first lieutenant.

These were among the darkest days of the Revolution—"the times that try men's souls," as Thomas Paine wrote. Things had gone badly for Washington and his army in New York. What had been a force of more than twenty thousand men in July had dwindled to a ragged band of less than eight thousand by the end of the year, and many of these soldiers were leaving the army. Now Washington's troops had retreated to Trenton, New Jersey, and he warned the Continental Congress that a battle to defend Philadelphia was approaching.

Panic gripped Philadelphia as shops closed and people hurried to leave the city. In desperate need of manpower, Washington called upon General Thomas Mifflin, who rounded up three battalions of Philadelphia Associators under John Cadwalader, Peale's old patron. The force of about a thousand men was ordered to advance to Trenton. Before leaving, Peale made efforts to ensure the safety of his family, locating a refuge for them in a house about twelve miles north of the city. Next he visited the home of each member of his company to find out what the family would need while the men were away, and then he made another list of the men's needs on active duty. His obvious concern for their welfare enabled him to pull together a company of eighty-one men. In Peale they found an officer not particularly good at enforcing strong discipline, but one who did his best to ensure their well-being.

No sooner had the militia arrived in Trenton than they were ordered to cross the Delaware River to the Pennsylvania side. British troops were approaching Trenton from the north, and Washington planned to use the river as his line of defense. After the militia crossed the river came the core of Washington's army, the "ragged Continentals" who had fought in the unsuccessful Boston and New York campaigns. A scene of mass confusion was played out in the dark of night, with watch fires on the riverbank casting eerie shadows, men shouting and cursing. As Peale later wrote, it was "the most hellish scene that I have ever beheld."

Anxiously he scanned the faces of the soldiers, hoping to spot his brother James and brother-in-law Nathaniel Ramsay. Both were members of the Maryland regiment that had fought in the bruising

New York campaign. To his great relief, he located them the next day but almost didn't recognize James, whose face was covered with sores. Peale looked after him until he was on the mend and found him a new uniform from the militia's supply.

The British troops arrived and occupied Trenton, from which they planned to move on to Philadelphia. But not yet. Winter campaigns presented great difficulties in those days, so British commander-in-chief Sir William Howe decided to wait—and in the meantime enjoy the social life of New York. Washington had assumed that Howe would want to strike a final blow while he had the advantage. When this did not happen, the American general decided to undertake a series of offensive thrusts. To succeed he needed the combined strength of his regular troops and the militia.

For two weeks they watched and waited. Peale used some of his time to paint miniatures of a few officers, as he had packed his art supplies with his other belongings when he left Philadelphia. In that rough-and-tumble military life, conditions were less than perfect for making art. But whenever there was a lull, out came his paints.

Washington was busy laying his plans, and on Christmas Eve, 1776, he made his now famous crossing of the Delaware to reoccupy Trenton. Although Peale did not take part in that event, he was not far away. Cadwalader's troops had been ordered to cross the river at Bristol and head for Trenton, ten miles away.

After a long, tiring march over muddy roads, they reached Trenton. There was no time to rest, however. Eight thousand British troops under Lord Cornwallis had been roused out of their winter quarters in New York and ordered by Howe to "bag the old fox." Washington, the old fox, had a few tricks up his sleeve, and in a brilliant maneuver he evaded Cornwallis and moved his army on to Princeton, twelve miles away.

Self-Portrait in Uniform, ca. 1777–1778.

American Philosophical Society.

Peale is wearing the uniform of the Philadelphia militia.

The militia units rarely made it to the front lines during the war, as they lacked the training and experience of the regular army. Their terms of enlistment were usually so short—in many cases less than a year—that by the time they had learned the ropes they were ready to go home. At the Battle of Princeton, however, Peale's militia unit unexpectedly played an important role.

General Hugh Mercer's Continentals were on the front line and met a fierce British bayonet charge. Armed only with muskets, they fled the field as their general lay on the ground mortally wounded.

By chance, Cadwalader's troops, including Peale's company, were nearby. Washington quickly brought them forward to charge the British regiment, but the redcoats broke the charge. Just when it looked as if all was lost, a Philadelphia militia captain brought up two four-pounder guns and pushed back the British attack. This enabled Washington to ride onto the field and rally his troops, including Cadwalader's men and New England Continental regiments.

On that day Lady Luck seemed to be on their side. As Peale later described the scene, they "stood the fire without regarding [cannon] Balls which whistled their thousand different notes around our heads, and what is very astonishing did little or no harm."

Washington's troops let loose one volley after another until finally the British abandoned their weapons and fled the field. "Huzzah!" shouted one of the American officers. "They fly! The day is our own!" All along the line a cheer went up.

The militia had covered itself with glory, but the men were bone-weary and hungry—too tired to fight and not at all pleased to hear the order to begin marching north. When they did finally stop to rest, Peale showed his awareness that an army marches on its stomach. In his diary he noted that he had gone to "a House farther in Town & purchased some Beef, which I got the good Woman to boil against I should call for it in the morning. And I got a small kettle full of Potatoes Boil'd where we lodged."

The next morning before sunrise, as the drums were sounding the call to begin marching again, Peale's company could be found sitting by the side of the road enjoying the hot meal he had prepared. When Washington rode by and noticed this jolly group still savoring their breakfast while others were on the move, he stopped for an explanation. Peale replied that he was simply providing his men with some much-needed nourishment. "Very well. March on as fast as you can," was the general's reply.

When the army stopped in northern New Jersey, Peale was able to put to good use his skills from old saddlery days. The long marches through mud and icy terrain had worn out the shoes of many soldiers. Some of them had even been forced to go barefoot in the wintry weather. Peale located some leather hides and set to work making moccasins for those most in need. Mindful of the cold, he made sure the fur was on the inside to keep their feet snug and warm.

There was good news for these war-weary soldiers. Cornwallis had withdrawn his forces from Trenton and New Brunswick and headed back to New York. Washington planned to remain at his winter quarters in Morristown, New Jersey, but it was time for Peale's company to march home on January 14, 1777. Their term of enlistment in the militia had ended.

Years later in his autobiography, Peale recalled his experience as a soldier:

> Peale was a thin, spare, pale-faced man, in appearance totally
> unfit to endure the fatigues of long marches, and lying on the cold

wet ground, sometimes covered with snow. Yet by temperance and by a forethought of providing for the worst that might happen, he endured this campaign better than many others whose appearance was more robust. He always carried a piece of dryed Beef and Bisquits in his Pocket, and Water in his Canteen, which he found, was much better than Rum.

Peale later served another term in the militia, but he was not involved in any more battles. Yet what he had experienced at Princeton, and later observed as the revolution continued, convinced him of the horrors of war. Others might seek the role of military hero, but he preferred to make his mark with a paintbrush.

10

I<small>F</small> P<small>EALE</small> <small>WAS NOT CUT OUT FOR THE LIFE OF A SOLDIER,</small> he was even less well suited for the world of politics. He had gotten a taste of it back in Maryland while campaigning for Samuel Chase. Political activity had led to trouble for him then, and in 1777 it brought new difficulties.

The Pennsylvania state constitution had been written a few months after the signing of the Declaration of Independence. Owing to the Revolution, it had been ordered into force without being ratified. The new constitution provided for a one-chamber legislature, to be directly elected by the people every year. A Supreme Executive Council, composed of twelve members—one from each county—was also to be elected by the people, and members of this body would elect the judiciary.

To the conservative Whigs in Philadelphia—the old colonial men of wealth and property such as financier Robert Morris—this form of government raised the specter of mob rule. They urged that a new convention be held to revise the constitution. What they proposed was a legislature made up of two chambers, an executive with veto power, and a judiciary that was not subject to popular control.

Peale sided with the so-called "Furious Whigs," who supported the constitution as it stood. Benjamin Franklin had given it his endorsement. There was no need for two chambers, he said; it didn't make any sense to hitch a horse to each end of the cart. Among the other prominent backers of the constitution were David Rittenhouse and Thomas Paine, whose fiery writings such as *Common Sense* had rallied colonists to the Revolution. Behind them stood tradesmen, artisans, and people of humble means who were being given a stronger voice in government.

Although this issue pitted the conservative "True Whigs" against the radical "Furious Whigs," both groups supported the cause for independence. Indeed, Robert Morris, a leader of the anticonstitutionalists, became known as the "financier of the Revolution" for his efforts to raise money for Washington's army.

The "Furious Whigs" formed a Whig Society, and at one of its meetings Peale found himself more deeply involved than he had intended. During the course of the meeting, several people were nominated to be chairman of the society but turned it down. In a remark to the person standing next to him, Peale said he "wondered why gentlemen should be so unwilling to take the trouble of only keeping order, in an assembly of their fellow Citizens."

The next thing he knew Peale was being nominated as chairman. How could he possibly refuse after the remark he had just made? It was the beginning of a chain of events he could never have imagined. As his autobiography states: "And from this accidental affair, the launching out into that dangerous and trouble-some Political Sea, subject to like troubles by every blast, and very often in contrary directions. . . . For the differences of opinion here made him Enemies in those, whom before he considered his best friends." Among that number were some of his old patrons.

Politics were put aside in June when it became known that the British were stirring in northern New Jersey and making plans to swoop down and occupy Philadelphia. Peale was promoted to the rank of captain in the Philadelphia brigade and set out for the front, although the city militia had not yet been called to active duty. Anxiety about his family's safety brought him back to Philadelphia during the ensuing months. Such leaves of absence were a privilege granted to militia officers.

Peale happened to be in Philadelphia on August 24 when an army of ten thousand Continental soldiers marched through, led by General Washington on horseback with the Marquis de Lafayette at his side. They were on their way to Wilmington, Delaware, to intercept British troops heading for Philadelphia from the south. It was a stirring sight to the crowds who lined the streets, and their hopes for victory were raised by this display of manpower.

Cheers for the Continentals soon turned to jeers for the Tories living in the city. The Executive Council sought to enforce mea-sures for the arrest of British loyalists. Peale was named to a com-mittee responsible for ferreting out Tories and obtaining pledges of loyalty.

Ironically, one of the people he had to confront was James Tilghman—the man who had helped him get a start in the saddlery business and then turned on him with the threat of prison. A similar fate now seemed to await Tilghman. Peale apparently remembered the man's good deeds rather than the bad and treated his onetime benefactor with consideration. This was often not the case in other places, where Tories were routinely tarred and feathered.

By mid-September, Philadelphia's Tories could breathe a little easier. Washington's army had been defeated in the Battle of Brandywine, at Chadds Ford, Pennsylvania. This made British occupation of Philadelphia all but certain. On September 25, 1777, General Howe and his troops marched into the city, where they were greeted enthusiastically by the Tories. The tables had turned, and woe betide any patriots who were still hanging around.

Peale's family managed to find a safe haven outside the city, thanks to his frantic last-minute efforts. Now it was time to rejoin his company. In early November, Washington moved his troops to Whitemarsh, thirteen miles from Philadelphia. There he planned to play a waiting game, taking a strong position close enough to the British lines to make them uneasy.

Winter set in with a numbing cold that froze the ground and seeped into the old decaying mill where Peale and his men were billeted. He had been placed in command of a picket guard, and one night, after coming off duty at a late hour, he fell asleep on a plank. It was so icy cold that he awakened a short time later and discovered that his right hand was numb. He massaged it with cold water and by morning had recovered some feeling in the hand, except for two fingers. More than two months passed before it returned to normal, and he could stop worrying that his career as a painter was over. By this time Peale's term of enlistment had ended, and he returned to his family.

The Peales' refuge in Bucks County, Pennsylvania, was not the safe haven they had hoped for. Loyalists roamed the countryside at night, raiding the homes of suspected Whigs and taking them prisoner. Many a night Peale took his gun and went off to sleep in the woods, covering himself with a blanket among the leaves. Rachel was soon to give birth to another child, so moving the family elsewhere was out of the question.

There was one place he was sure to be safe from these roving bands. In mid-December 1777, Washington had moved his army from Whitemarsh to Valley Forge. Peale's brother-in-law and good friend, Nathaniel Ramsay, was now a lieutenant colonel and could offer shelter in the house where he was posted. Rachel pleaded with him to go there to relieve her anxiety.

At Valley Forge, Peale rustled up some business painting miniatures of the officers and their wives encamped there for the winter. He also began to make portrait studies of some of the officers on small squares of canvas. From this work the idea was born of one day establishing a gallery of portraits of the men who had played an important role in America's struggle for independence. At camp he occasionally had dinner with Washington and struck up a friendship with Lafayette, enjoying the opportunity to practice his French.

Late winter and spring brought some good news. On February 22, 1778, Rachel gave birth to another son, who was named Rembrandt. Then, lifting everyone's spirits, the word came that France had entered into an alliance with the Americans. With an infusion of money and manpower from this powerful nation, hopes of victory skyrocketed. By June the British had left Philadelphia and were heading back to New York. Close behind them were more than three thousand Tories who realized they would no longer be welcome in the city.

The traffic also began to move in the opposite direction, as Whigs flocked back to their homes. With fewer worries at their doorstep, they could now turn their attention to political battles.

The conservatives renewed their attacks on the state constitution, which was promptly defended by the Furious Whigs. Peale once again was in the midst of the fray and soon found himself involved in a particularly unpleasant task. He was appointed one of the commissioners responsible for seizing the homes and property of Tories and preparing them for sale or auction. Commissioners often had to be the judges of whether or not a person had been disloyal, and this sometimes meant sorting out truth from falsehood if a person was unjustly accused of being disloyal. No man could have been less temperamentally suited to the job than Peale, who later described it as "the most difficult, laborious and disagreeable task I have ever undertaken."

In January 1779 he received an assignment more in keeping with his talents. The Supreme Executive Council of Pennsylvania commissioned Peale to paint a portrait of General Washington. The artist threw himself into his work, well aware that this public commission would be important for his career. It was also a portrait that had special meaning for him personally, as he chose to paint the victorious general as he might have looked after the Battle of Princeton. The artist rejected the stiff formality of most military portraits. Washington was depicted on the field at the end of the battle, one hand resting on a cannon and surrounded by symbols of the British defeat. The portrait was a great popular success, and during the next few years Peale received numerous commissions for copies of the painting.

The political war in Philadelphia, however, conspired to keep Peale out of his studio. The conservatives lost the battle for a new constitutional convention and formed a Republican Society to strike back. This led the Furious Whigs to found a Constitutional Society, with Peale as chairman.

George Washington at Princeton, 1779.

The Pennsylvania Academy of the Fine Arts.

Gift of the exchange of Elizabeth Wharton McKean Estate.

It was a period of great hardship for many people in the city. Owing to wartime shortages of food and clothing, prices rose and goods became unaffordable for poor people. The Furious Whigs supported price controls and other measures to curb the runaway profits being made by many merchants. The wealthy and influential Robert Morris was a particular target of the more radical Whigs such as Thomas Paine.

Unlike many of his fellow Whigs, Peale tried to steer a more moderate course, but he was unable to curb the rising tide of radical fury. Although he tried to put a stop to some of the violence, he was not always successful. The reluctant politician was even sometimes physically attacked on the street by conservatives. Friends urged him to carry a firearm, but he refused. After a particularly nasty run-in, one of his friends gave him a wooden cane, which he named Hercules. On one occasion he used it to drive off an attacker and then began to carry it whenever he went out on foot.

In the fall of 1779 Peale was a candidate for the state assembly on the Independent Constitutional ticket. He and his running mate won in a landslide, defeating Robert Morris, whose conservative backers included John Cadwalader and John Dickinson. Among Peale's first friends and patrons in Philadelphia, they were now aligned against him.

During his term in office Peale served as chairman or held membership on thirty different legislative committees. That year the assembly passed a statute for the gradual abolition of slavery in Pennsylvania, which freed all the children of slaves born within the state. Peale was himself the owner of several slaves, which he had brought north with him from Maryland. By this time he had come to believe that "the very idea of slavery is horrible" and determined to release his adult slaves as soon as they could support themselves.

In the election the following year, the political pendulum swung to the right. Robert Morris and the conservatives won, promising not to tinker with the state constitution. Peale was not sorry to leave the political arena, vowing never to venture into it again. He would spend the next two years in a state of nervous exhaustion—the bitter harvest of his public service.

CHAPTER

11

THE BEST MEDICINE FOR PEALE'S LOW SPIRITS PROVED TO be the news of victory in the war for independence. As he recalled years later in a letter to his daughter Angelica, "It was to me like waking from a dreadful dream. I could scarcely believe my senses that it was not a dream and dangers past; my joy was great to know that I could lay me down to rest, without fear of alarm before morning."

The defeat of Lord Cornwallis's troops at Yorktown, Virginia, in October 1781 touched off a round of celebrations in Philadelphia. Holidays like the Fourth of July and other special occasions were usually observed with what were called "illuminations." Instead of closing their shutters at night, people would leave them open and place candles in the windows. The light coming from the row-houses cast a warm glow over the pavements, where throngs of people would be strolling.

For this very special victory celebration, an even better idea occurred to a young Frenchman then living in the city. He removed the sashes in two windows of his house and replaced them with transparent pictures of patriotic subjects, which were lighted from behind with candles. (Transparent pictures were usually painted on window-shade cloth primed with wax and turpentine.)

The effect was striking and immediately sparked Peale's imagination. By nightfall of the following evening he was ready with his own extravaganza. All the members of the Peale household had pitched in, especially his brother James. Their windows displayed transparent pictures that included portraits of the triumphant leaders of the Yorktown campaign, Washington and his French ally Count Rochambeau. In a third-floor window, in letters large enough to read from the street, were the words "For Our Allies, Huzza! Huzza! Huzza!"

Word spread quickly of the great show at Peale's house. "And the whole," he later wrote, "made so brilliant a display, that the People from all parts of the City came and so crowded the streets that if a Basket should be thrown out it could not meet with a vacancy to get to the ground within a considerable distance from the House." The presentation was such a huge success that Peale and his brother followed it up with several others, each more spectacular than the one before.

Peale did not yet realize that he had taken the first step toward building an audience for his work that had little to do with the wealthy private patrons who had supported him in the past. In Philadelphia many of them had turned their backs on him because of his political activities. Others would take their place to some extent, but in the years ahead Peale's success would depend on the general public.

The Accident in Lombard Street, 1787.

Courtesy Library of Congress.

The house in the foreground is Peale's.

A further move in that direction was the project inspired by painting miniatures of the officers at Valley Forge. Peale dreamed of creating a Gallery of Great Men, filled with portraits of the heroes of the Revolution. This would include not just General Washington and officers who had led their men into battle but also foreign allies and patriots on the home front who had helped win the war. To Peale, it was not just a picture gallery but a way to inspire his fellow citizens to live up to the highest ideals of a republican form of government. It would also be a legacy to future generations.

Standing in the way of this venture was Peale's usual problem, a lack of money. The previous summer he had bought a large brick house at Third and Lombard streets, which was not yet paid for. And there were many more mouths to feed in the Peale household. Raphaelle, Angelica, and Rembrandt had a new baby brother, born in 1780, named Titian Ramsay Peale. Also under Peale's wing were the two teenage children of his sister Elizabeth and her husband, Robert Polk, both of whom had died during the war.

In the summer of 1782 he decided not to wait any longer and went ahead with plans to build an addition to his house for the gallery. He struck a deal with the carpenters that would allow him to pay for their labor when he could afford it. If he ran short of cash, work would stop until he had earned enough money for them to start again. To keep his business humming, Peale offered a half-price rate for his portrait miniatures. There were enough customers to keep both him and his carpenters busy without interruption.

By fall the first public picture gallery in America—and the first to have a skylight—was ready to open its doors. Hanging in the long, narrow room were some thirty portraits, ranging from full-length pictures of Washington and the French diplomat Conrad

Alexandre Gérard to smaller portraits of Lafayette, Baron von Steuben, and other foreign and American officers. Among the civilian patriots were Robert Morris and Thomas Paine—archenemies in Pennsylvania politics but now side by side on the gallery wall.

Over the next two years Peale added a dozen more portraits to the gallery. Although he charged no admission fees, he hoped to earn some money by making copies of the portraits on commission. At first the gallery attracted considerable attention, but interest gradually faded and few commissions were received. Nonetheless the gallery brought Peale a new measure of esteem in Philadelphia— even if it didn't win back many of his influential former patrons.

The postwar years brought hard times for many people, as the young nation struggled to build a strong economy. Peale's debts were piling up. His earlier bargain rates for miniatures were now working against him; people wanted a similar half-price rate for his larger portraits. The artist's rocky financial state was described in his letter to Dr. Benjamin Rush requesting payment for a picture he had painted:

> When a person is in Cash, the people of Maryland use the phrase, such a one is in Blast. If he is without Money, then he is out of Blast. . . . I am out of Blast. My Building has made me miserably poor. If it is convenient to you to assist me into Blast you will very much oblige your very
>
> Humble Servt.

Financial cares were put aside in 1783 after the signing of the peace treaty with Britain that formally ended the war. The Pennsylvania General Assembly decided that this called for "public demonstrations of joy," among them the erection of a triumphal

Conrad Alexandre Gérard, 1779.

Courtesy, Independence National Historical Park.

arch in Philadelphia decorated with illuminated paintings. The committee agreed that there was no better person to handle this project than "the ingenious Captain Peale."

While the carpenters were busy constructing the framework for the fifty-by-forty-foot wooden arch on Market Street, Peale set to work on the thirteen pictures and other details. The man of the hour, George Washington, was of course depicted, along with symbols of France and tributes to the militia and government of Pennsylvania. Crowning the arch were statues of Justice, Prudence, Fortitude, and Temperance. Peale's elaborate design left an empty space in the center of the parapet, which was reserved for a large figure representing Peace. This was to be placed on the roof of an adjacent building and, with the aid of a mechanism Peale had rigged up, would slide into position on the night of the celebration. This would signal the lighting of more than a thousand lamps inside the arch and, in a grand finale, trigger a display of hundreds of rockets, or fireworks.

On the night of January 22, 1784, huge crowds gathered on Market Street in front of the arch. Peale and his son Raphaelle scurried up to the adjacent roof, ready to send the statue of Peace on her descent to the arch. Unfortunately, the rockets had been set too close to the highly flammable paintings, and when the first one went off, it ignited these works. They burned instantly, and the blaze touched off the rest of the rockets, which rained down on the horrified spectators. One person was killed, and several were injured, including Peale, whose clothes caught fire. Jumping to the ground, he broke several ribs but managed to put out the flames and stagger home.

Despite the fire, the framework of the arch was still intact, so that only new paintings were needed. The assembly decided to restage the spectacle in May—this time without the rockets. To his great dismay, Peale found he had to bear much of the expense for this. As a result he was seriously "out of Blast" when his son Rubens was born in May.

Peale's money problems were eased when he received three important public commissions during this period for portraits of George Washington. These were also a major boost to his reputation as an artist. But he was disappointed that the Gallery of Great Men was not attracting enough visitors. Then from London came word of a new kind of spectacle that struck Peale as just the ticket to bring crowds to the gallery who would be willing to pay an admission fee. In 1780, at the Drury Lane Theatre in London, Philip James de Loutherbourg had introduced pictures that moved and changed color by means of lighting effects. Peale realized that they had much in common with the transparent pictures he had done earlier. What he didn't know already, he was certain he could work out if he put his mind to it.

For months he worked feverishly on the project, barely taking time to eat and sleep. In the fall of 1784 a room was added to the end of the long gallery to provide space for all the equipment; the audience would sit in the gallery to watch the show. On May 19, 1785, he was finally ready to announce the opening performance in the *Pennsylvania Packet*: "Mr. Peale respectfully informs the public that with great labour and expense, he hath prepared a number of *perspective views*, with changeable effects, imitating nature in various *movements*." In London the inventor had called it the Eidophusikon (meaning "image of nature"). Peale chose a simpler term, settling on "moving pictures"—the first use of the term in America.

The two-hour show consisted of five scenes and provided a large sampling of what Mother Nature had to offer—from dawn breaking over the countryside to rainstorms with thunder and lightning. A more imaginative depiction showed Lucifer's city, based on a description in John Milton's "Paradise Lost." Peale later added an action-packed depiction of the famous naval battle of the Revolution, in which John Paul Jones's ship *Bonhomme Richard* captured the British vessel *Serapis*. His special effects included wooden waves that moved mechanically in the foreground, with small pipes inside them sending up sprays of water. All of this was accompanied by sound effects offstage, in addition to music and dramatic readings.

It was a smashing success, but not for long. Creating the various parts of the show took a lot of time and money, which made it difficult for Peale to change the program often. However much they enjoyed it, viewers wanted to see something different the next time they paid admission. The moving pictures continued to be shown during the next few years, but less often, and in 1790 they were sold. By then Peale had embarked on the most ambitious project of his life.

CHAPTER

· —————————— ·

12

O N JULY 18, 1786, AN UNUSUAL ANNOUNCEMENT APPEARED in the *Pennsylvania Packet*:

MR. PEALE, ever desirous to please and entertain the Public, will make a part of his House a Repository for Natural Curiosities— The Public he hopes will thereby be gratified in the sight of many of the Wonderful Works of Nature which are now closeted and but seldom seen.

There had been other, small-scale exhibits and collections of such materials in Philadelphia, but none would equal Peale's museum. What led him to make this leap into the world of natural science, a field so far removed from his career as an artist?

Money, of course, had something to do with it. Ever on the look-out for ways to support his large family, Peale first got the idea in the summer of 1783. He was asked by a local doctor to make thirty or forty drawings of some mastodon bones that had been found in Kentucky. This discovery had caused great excitement in the scientific community. For Peale's convenience, the huge bones of this prehistoric creature were brought to his gallery, where he kept them while making the drawings. It soon became obvious that visitors were fascinated by the bones. This included the artist's brother-in-law Nathaniel Ramsay, who declared that "he would have gone twenty miles to behold such a collection." Here was something, he told Peale, that would offer more financial rewards than painting.

The museum that Peale established would end up being far more than a collection of fossils and oddities. Even its founder did not at first envision what was to become the first scientifically organized museum of natural history in America. Like every other project that captured Peale's imagination, all his energies went into it. In his autobiography he described it as

> a work so difficult that had he known what he was about to undertake, he would perhaps have rather put his hand into the fire. But such is the bewitching study of Nature that it expands the mind to embrace object after object, and the desire is still fed in an endless maze of contemplation of the wondrous works of Creation.

What Peale didn't know about natural history—which was quite a lot, given his lack of formal education—he set about learning by reading every book on the subject he could find. Among them were the works of the Swedish botanist Charles Linnaeus, whose system of classifying plant and animal life would be used in the museum.

Formally named the Philadelphia Museum, it was referred to by most people in the city and farther afield as Peale's Museum. In his day, museums as we now know them did not exist. What few institutions there were, such as the British Museum in London, were largely the preserve of scholars. The general public had only limited access, and certainly no effort was made to educate them. At Peale's museum, anyone with the twenty-five-cent price of admission was welcome to come in and learn in his "Great School of Nature," as he called it.

Those who did so wanted to be entertained as well, and Peale never lost sight of that fact. But as a true son of the eighteenth-century Enlightenment, or Age of Reason—influenced by French thinkers such as Rousseau and Voltaire—he placed great importance on education. "The attainment of Happiness, Individual as well as Public, depends on the cultivation of the human mind," he wrote in a letter to his friend and fellow believer Thomas Jefferson (who would later become president of the museum's board of visitors).

Benjamin Franklin encouraged Peale in his plans for the museum, as did the American Philosophical Society, which Franklin founded in Philadelphia in 1743. Also helpful to Peale was Philadelphia's active scientific community, whose expertise he could tap.

The museum's collection grew rapidly. Among the first donors was Franklin, who gave the corpse of his French angora cat. Washington contributed a pair of golden pheasants, given to him as live animals by Lafayette. Later, as the museum became better known, specimens came from many different parts of the world. After the Lewis and Clark expedition of 1803–1804 to the territory west of the Mississippi River, then-President Jefferson arranged for specimens acquired in their travels to go to Peale's museum.

Sea captains returning to port in Philadelphia brought creatures

Benjamin Franklin, 1785.

The Pennsylvania Academy of the Fine Arts. Joseph and Sarah Harrison Collection.

Thomas Jefferson, 1791.

Courtesy, Independence National Historical Park.

from more distant lands, such as a llama, an antelope, an ape, and monkeys. Live animals were kept outside in a kind of open-air zoo until they eventually died and were ready to be preserved for the museum collection. It was quite an assortment of pets for the Peale children.

One of Peale's first challenges was to find an effective way to preserve the specimens. Few sources of instruction were available, so he had to devise his own techniques. After many experiments, he settled on using an arsenic solution for the birds and smaller animals and bichloride of mercury for the larger specimens. These did the job well but were highly poisonous substances that could endanger the health of those who came in contact with them.

The purpose of his museum, Peale stated, was "to bring into one view a world in miniature." With the eye of an artist, he succeeded in making it a visual treat for visitors. Instead of just putting the bird specimens in glass cases, he painted a watercolor landscape for the inside of each case that showed the bird's natural habitat and then placed it on a branch or rock posed in a lifelike manner. Peale's innovative habitat displays would become standard museum practice in modern times. For some of the larger animals, he often achieved a more lifelike appearance by first making a wood sculpture detailed enough to show the muscles and then stretching the animal skin over it.

Not overlooked in this "world in miniature" was *Homo sapiens* (humankind). Along the entire length of the main gallery, above the display of birds, were Peale's portraits of great men. In what had once been the moving-picture room he built a grotto with imitation rocks for reptiles and marine specimens.

The Peale children had the run of the museum, which became more of a school for them than the one where they received a for-

Self-Portrait with Rachel and Angelica Peale, ca. 1788.

The Museum of Fine Arts, Houston.

The Bayou Bend Collection, gift of Miss Ima Hogg.

mal education. Peale gave them all lessons in drawing and painting, and the boys were taught to use the tools in his carpentry shop. Unlike many people of his day, he believed that daughters as well as sons should be educated. Women were just as capable of great accomplishments as men, he stated, provided they were not confined to "affairs which allow no time for them to devote to the arduous pursuits of science."

At a time when iron discipline was usually imposed on children, Peale shared Rousseau's view that they should be led "to paths of Virtue with a Chain of Flowers." In other words, parents should not rule by the rod but instead persuade their children to do good by setting a good example themselves and providing a happy domestic environment.

To support his family, even after opening the museum, Peale was still very much involved with portrait painting. This was the work that paid all the bills. The family now had two new daughters, both named for Italian women artists: Sophonisba Angusciola, born in 1786, and Rosalba Carriera, in 1788.

With wealthy patrons still not knocking at his door in Philadelphia, Peale decided to take the advice of his longtime benefactor John Beale Bordley and seek work in Maryland. Although this meant much travel back and forth to Philadelphia, he obtained many commissions and produced some of his most accomplished portraits.

By 1790 the museum's reputation was growing, even if it was not yet on a sound financial footing. But personal tragedies soon shattered Peale's world. His wife, Rachel, had never quite recovered from the birth of Rosalba, and she then contracted tuberculosis, which led to her death in April 1790. Within the year Peale also mourned the deaths of tiny Rosalba, his mother, and Peggy Durgan.

Benjamin and Eleanor Ridgely Laming, 1788.

National Gallery of Art. Gift of Morris Schapiro.

These women—Rachel most of all—had created the domestic harmony in which he thrived.

The need for female companionship (as well as a mother for his six children) led him to look for a new wife. In 1791 he found a likely prospect right in his museum. Elizabeth DePeyster, visiting from New York, was with a group viewing the collection. When they stopped to rest and began singing, Peale heard her lovely voice. To the music-loving Peale, it indicated "a harmonious mind." Although only twenty-five years old, she had a "serious motherly appearance" that made her seem more mature. Within a few weeks of their meeting, he proposed, and they were married in May 1791.

Betsy DePeyster Peale soon found herself caring for six youngsters ranging in age from five (Sophy) to seventeen (Raphaelle). A plump, tidy woman with a sense of order and decorum inherited from her Dutch ancestors, she must have wondered more than once what she had gotten herself into. Peale's permissive views on child-rearing were quite different from the ideas that shaped her own upbringing. And outside in the yard was a menagerie of wild animals that sometimes raised a ruckus. Even the kitchen was not her private domain. It often did double duty as a laboratory, where specimens were prepared amid odors that were less than pleasing.

By the early 1790s the museum was running out of space to house the growing collection. In 1794 Peale accepted an offer from the American Philosophical Society to move his museum, as well as his family, into the newly built Philosophical Hall. This stronger connection with the society seemed likely to confer more prestige on the museum, and he hoped it would also help in his efforts to win public financial support. Moreover, the building was in a more central location, near the Statehouse (now Independence Hall).

Always on the alert to promote his ventures, Peale turned the move into a spectacle, as his autobiography describes:

> To take advantage of public curiosity, he contrived to make a very considerable parade of the articles, especially of those which was large. And as Boys generally are fond of parade, he collected all the boys of the neighbourhood, & he began a range of them at the head of which was carried on men's shoulders the American Buffalo—then followed the Panthers, Tyger Catts and a long string of Animals of smaller size carried by the boys.

The live animals also moved to Philosophical Hall, where they were kept in a fenced area near the building. Atop the hall, a large cage held a bald eagle who was as friendly as a puppy. Whenever it caught sight of Peale walking in the yard, it would sound out a greeting to him.

With new, larger quarters, Peale began to devote more of his time and energy to the museum. Later that year he announced in the newspaper that he was retiring from portrait painting in order to manage his museum. But he assured the public that there was no shortage of Peales to take his place, recommending his sons Rembrandt and Raphaelle.

It was largely to advance his sons' careers that Peale played a leading role in founding the Columbianum in December 1794. While in London he had benefited from membership in the Society of Artists, and he believed that a professional organization of this type was needed to advance the interests of artists in America. It would provide training for them as well as a place where their work could be exhibited. Unfortunately, owing to disagreements

The Staircase Group, 1795.

Philadelphia Museum of Art. The George W. Elkins Collection.

among the artists over its goals, the Columbianum lasted only long enough to present one exhibition in 1795.

Both Raphaelle and Rembrandt showed their work, as did the elder Peale, who proved to be not quite as "retired" from painting as he had previously stated. *The Staircase Group*—destined to become one of his most famous paintings—depicts Raphaelle and Titian climbing a staircase. The tall narrow work was set into a doorway with an actual wooden step at the base of the painted steps. At first glance, it fooled the eye so that viewers thought they were seeing real live boys. Rembrandt told the story that George Washington was among those who were tricked, as he "bowed politely to the painted figures."

If there was anything to signify Peale's switch from art to science, it was perhaps the birth of a son in 1794 who was named after Charles Linnaeus rather than a painter. The following year another son was born, and this time, when it came to choosing his name, the members of the Philosophical Society got into the act. At a meeting they unanimously voted to name him Franklin after their founder, who had died in 1790.

In 1798, at the age of eighteen, Titian Ramsay Peale died of yellow fever. During that era, little was known about the cause of the disease nor how to control it, so that the death rate was high in the epidemics that occurred regularly during the summer months. Titian had been his father's chief assistant at the museum and a naturalist of great promise. Of all the Peale children, he probably would have been the one most involved in the great adventure his father embarked on in 1801.

CHAPTER

13

O N June 5, 1801, Charles Willson Peale stepped aboard a stagecoach heading for New York. Now sixty years old, he was as excited as a boy of ten about what he might find at his destination. He had learned that a farmer in the Hudson Valley town of Newburgh had dug up some large fossil bones. What a boon to his museum these would be! Visitors were sure to come in droves to see the remains of a giant prehistoric creature.

But it was not just a case of show business for Peale. He knew that scientific knowledge would be increased by a study of the remains of an animal that had never been seen while alive. Scattered bones had turned up in various places from time to time, notably the ones discovered in Kentucky that he had drawn some years earlier. There was great curiosity among scientists about this mysterious creature, which was referred to as the "great incognitum" (unknown), or more commonly the "mammoth." No one had yet found enough of the bones to assemble a skeleton and get a better idea of what the animal looked like.

When Peale arrived at John Masten's farm and saw the bones, he realized what a find it was. Although some important parts were missing, and others were in poor condition, it was nonetheless the largest cache of bones ever found in one place. Masten had discovered them while digging for shell marl (used as fertilizer) in a water-filled pit. The bones had been carelessly removed and dragged back to the farmer's granary, where he had been exhibiting them to curious visitors for a small fee.

Peale got his permission to make life-size drawings of the bones, deciding not to broach the subject of buying them right away. Later, when the subject came up, Masten turned down his offer of two hundred dollars for the bones already dug up and another hundred dollars for the right to do more digging. That was all Peale could afford to spend, and he was in despair at the thought of losing them. Finally the farmer agreed to his terms, and Peale wrote to his wife that "my heart jumpt with joy."

The bones were packed in barrels and crates and shipped to Philadelphia. The thigh bone was so large that it didn't fit in any container, so Peale took it with him to New York—a piece of carry-on luggage that must have turned many heads. While visiting at the home of his brother-in-law John DePeyster, who was lending him most of the money for the purchase, Peale got a taste of the excitement the bones had generated. According to his diary, "The Vice President of the United States [Aaron Burr] and a considerable number of Ladies and Gentlemen came to see the Bones, the news of them must have flew like wild fire, for upwards of 80 persons came to see that evening."

Back in Philadelphia, when all the bones had been safely delivered to Philosophical Hall, Peale was able to inspect them more closely in preparation for reconstructing the skeleton. Although the lower jaw and upper part of the head were missing, the skeleton was almost complete. It was clear that these were the bones of one animal. And since the missing parts might still be buried in the marl pit, a new search was vital.

Peale turned for financial help to the American Philosophical Society, which had long been interested in acquiring a complete skeleton of the "great incognitum." Thomas Jefferson, who had been elected president of the society in 1797, had been studying the subject for years. On July 24, 1801, the society unanimously voted to give Peale a four-month loan of five hundred dollars. The first organized scientific expedition in the United States could now proceed.

When Peale returned to the Masten farm, his first priority was to find a way to set up and power the operation to drain some twelve feet of water from the pit. The use of hand pumps was one possibility, but he came up with a more ingenious idea. A rotating chain of buckets, hanging over the pit from a tall wooden tripod, was to be powered by men walking inside a huge millwheel. The mechanism worked so well that the water was low enough to start digging on the second day, according to Rembrandt, who was assisting his father.

There was no shortage of volunteers to walk inside the wheel. Hundreds of people had turned up to watch the operation, and many of them were eager to play a part. Peale also hired twenty-five men to do the digging, paying each of them $1.12 a day—considered top wages at the time.

As the men dug deeper and deeper in the pit, the soft banks

began to give way. It soon became necessary to abandon this site, but at least some bones of the foot and other parts had been found. Still missing, however, was the part Peale wanted most—the lower jaw. Not ready to give up, he moved on to two nearby sites. At one he found the scattered remains of a skeleton, but in very poor condition. Then at the final site he got lucky. His crew of diggers unearthed a nearly complete skeleton. The upper part of the head was missing, but he had found a complete lower jaw.

The expedition, which lasted five months, was the crowning achievement of Peale's career in natural science. His name would go down in the annals of paleontology (the study of fossils and ancient life forms). However, it was as an artist that he left a more dramatic record of his great adventure. In his painting *Exhumation of the Mastodon*, the great wheel-and-bucket apparatus is the central image. A tense moment is depicted when a thunderstorm has threatened to flood the pit and force him to end the search. The men continued to dig, and luckily the storm passed by. More than seventy-five people are shown in the painting, including many members of Peale's family. Here the artist departed from the facts, as Rembrandt was the only other Peale on the scene; it was simply Peale's way of making his entire family part of this exciting moment in his life.

Digging up the bones had been an impressive feat, but even more challenging was the task of assembling and mounting the skeletons. Only two of them were complete enough to be assembled, and this occupied Peale and Rembrandt's time for the next three months. They were assisted by sculptor William Rush and Moses Williams, Peale's former slave, who now worked in the museum.

The bones of each skeleton were kept separate, for, as

The Exhumation of the Mastodon, 1806–1808.

The Peale Museum, Baltimore City Life Museums.

Rembrandt stated, "It would not be proper to incorporate into one skeleton any other than bones belonging to it." When bones were missing, the Peales used carved wood replicas and carefully marked these man-made parts—practices widely used in museums today.

Later scientific study showed that the reconstruction was not entirely accurate. The addition of cartilage to the ribs made the creature look taller than it actually was. Also, the tusks were incorrectly pointed downward rather than up—a mistake they later corrected.

The Peales' work was nonetheless of major importance. Never before had such a specimen been assembled and mounted. It became the talk of the scientific world and the subject of much study in both America and Europe. Previously, the general name "mammoth" had been given to such huge mammals, which were thought to be related to the elephant. In 1806 the leading French scientist, Georges Cuvier, identified the animal found by Peale as a mastodon, based on the rounded shape of its teeth. He concluded that it had features of both the elephant and the hippopotamus and was therefore an entirely different genus of extinct mammal.

Peale's discovery had upset the theory known as the "great chain of being," which held that all of life was connected from the moment of creation and would exist forever in a harmonious relationship. Here, for the first time, was evidence that a species could become extinct.

In late December 1801 Peale was ready to exhibit one of the skeletons at Philosophical Hall. With his usual flair for publicity, he advertised it as "the ninth wonder of the world." The public eagerly lined up, quite willing to pay a separate admission fee of fifty cents just to visit the "Mammoth Room." There they gaped with amazement at a creature more than seventeen feet long from

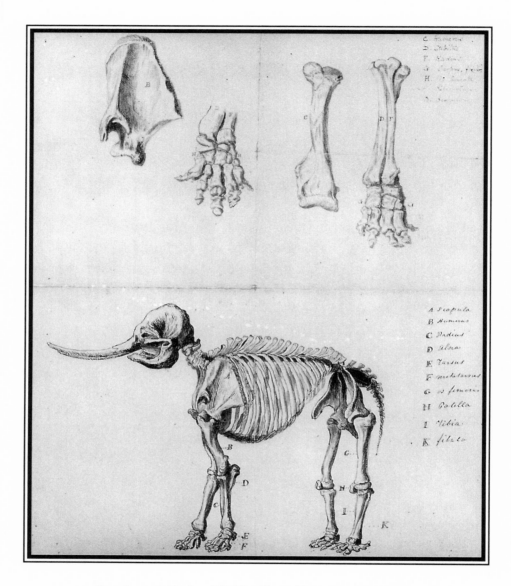

Rembrandt Peale, *Working Sketch of the Mastodon*, 1801.

American Philosophical Society.

tusk to tail, which stood eleven feet high at the shoulder and nine feet at the hips. The skeleton weighed a thousand pounds; the lower jaw alone weighed sixty-three pounds, a single tooth four pounds and ten ounces.

The exhibition set off a wave of "mammoth fever" throughout the country. In Philadelphia a baker sold a "mammoth bread"; one newspaper reported a "mammoth egg-eater . . . [who] swallowed 42 eggs in ten minutes, together with the shells!!!"

All of the hoopla gave Peale the idea that it might be profitable to send the second skeleton on a European tour. Rembrandt was to take charge and also spend some time studying art while he was abroad. Accompanying him would be seventeen-year-old Rubens, who was being groomed by his father for a managerial position in the museum.

Rembrandt decided these momentous events called for a party unlike any his guests had ever attended. Thirteen gentlemen were invited to sit down to dinner at a round walnut table placed under the ribs of the mastodon. To serenade them, John Hawkins's Patent Portable Grand Piano was set against the mastodon's hind legs. Glasses were raised and various toasts offered, among them, "To the arts and sciences: nursed in a genial soil, and fostered with tender care may their honour prove as *durable* as the *bower* which surrounds us."

14

WITH THE MASTODON IN PLACE, PEALE'S ALREADY CROWDED museum was now bursting at the seams. Clearly a larger space than Philosophical Hall was needed, and he was quick to realize there was no better time to solicit government aid. The interest of the general public, as well as the scientific world's response to his finding and assembling the mastodon, had brought new prestige to the museum.

In 1802 Peale submitted a proposal for the "National establishment" of his museum to President Jefferson. In his reply the president wrote that he, too, wished the museum "could be made public property," but said he doubted that Congress would be in favor of the idea. He explained that most members of Congress did not believe that the Constitution gave them authority to use public money for anything not specifically cited in that document.

With hopes for federal support dimmed, Peale turned to the

Pennsylvania state legislature. He had his eye on the Statehouse in Philadelphia, unoccupied since the legislature's move to Lancaster in 1799. His efforts were successful, and in March 1802 he was granted use of the upper floors of the main building and tower, as well as the first-floor east room (except on Election Day).

When the museum reopened in its new home in June of that year, a bigger and more beautiful assortment of exhibits was unveiled to visitors. The main gallery on the second floor, known as the Long Room, extended one hundred feet across the entire length of the building. Along one wall, in habitat settings as before, were the birds in glass cases. Installed above them were Peale's portraits of great men framed in gold. In 1808 there were eighty-eight portraits, and the number grew rapidly thereafter when Peale returned to painting. Also prominently displayed here were his large portraits of George Washington and Conrad Alexandre Gérard, along with *The Staircase Group*. On the opposite side of the room from the birds were cases containing four thousand specimens of insects and also a large mineral collection. To permit a close inspection of small insects, Peale set up an adjustable compound microscope with a revolving lens.

A separate Marine Room offered displays of reptiles and fish. In one exhibit a lens focused on the poison ducts in a snake's fangs. Peale sometimes provided a show of his own by handling some of the live snakes that were also on view.

According to a guidebook to the museum published in 1804, the thirty-foot-long Quadruped Room held more than 190 four-footed specimens. Among them were a buffalo, grizzly bear, hyena, antelope, and llama. Peale liked to study animals while they were alive, which helped him to create more lifelike poses when it came time to preserve them. There was still no shortage of live animals outside in the Statehouse yard, including monkeys, bears, a cageful of parrots, and Peale's old friend the bald eagle.

The museum had a number of preserved animal oddities that usually stopped visitors in their tracks. Dead or alive, a cow with five legs, six feet, and two tails was bound to attract attention. However, Peale shied away from exhibiting too many freaks of nature, which he feared would detract from the museum's serious scientific and educational goals.

The mastodon remained in Philosophical Hall in a room of its own until 1810, when it was moved over to the Statehouse. Also on display at Philosophical Hall were artifacts from Native American tribes, Polynesia, and the Far East, as well as a collection of machines and inventions and casts of antique statues.

For Peale, the harmony in the natural world had its counterpart in music. He purchased an organ for the museum, and recitals became a regular feature of the evening illumination. On these occasions the museum was lit by whale-oil lamps (and later gaslight), a novel experience for visitors, who were able to enjoy being in a brilliantly lit room after sundown.

With the death of his wife, Betsy, in February 1804, Peale's domestic harmony was shattered. Their thirteen years of marriage had produced five surviving children—Charles Linnaeus, Benjamin Franklin, Sybilla, Titian Ramsay II, and Elizabeth. Peale was again a widower with a flock of youngsters to raise.

As before, work and his diverse interests helped him to lay aside his cares. And after years of devoting most of his time to the museum, he picked up his neglected palette and brushes and began to paint. This renewed interest was related to his efforts to help found the Pennsylvania Academy of the Fine Arts in 1805. Ten years earlier his hopes for such an institution had been dashed when the short-lived Columbianum failed. This time, instead of warring artists, the founders were mostly businessmen and lawyers. If their views were more conservative, their bank accounts were larger and able to provide the funding for a school of art and an exhibition gallery. Until 1810 Peale served as a director of the academy, which to this day is an important museum and teaching institution in Philadelphia.

Despite his ability to immerse himself in his work, Peale was at heart a domestic creature who thrived on the affection and support of his family. That most definitely included a wife, and once again he found a new mate right in his museum. She was a middle-aged Quaker lady named Hannah Moore, plain in appearance but serene and cheerful—qualities she would need as the stepmother of five lively youngsters. News of the wedding in August 1805 was reported to Thomas Jefferson by the architect Benjamin Latrobe: "Peale is again married, I think. This is his third ticket in the lottery of marriage."

Hannah Moore proved to be a winning ticket. She quickly won the hearts of the children at home as well as the grown-up offspring from Peale's first marriage. Her warmth and devotion to her husband contributed to the remarkable creativity he displayed in the following years.

During this period Rubens Peale assumed greater responsibility for management of the museum. It was flourishing in its new quarters, bringing the founder a level of prosperity he had never known before. Peale was now able to devote more time to his varied interests. He took special delight in painting, but his boundless curiosity and energy made him incapable of focusing on just one thing.

His early days as a jack-of-all-trades had fueled his interest in inventing mechanical devices and practical objects. In 1797 he received the first U.S. patent for his design of an arched wooden bridge, and he and Raphaelle that same year patented an improved type of fireplace with a damper above and sliding shutter for closing the front, which allowed the fire to be controlled like a stove.

From 1803 to 1808 a new apparatus claimed much of Peale's attention. In the days before photocopying machines or even typewriters, the only way to get a copy of a letter or document was to write it out all over again. The polygraph, invented by Peale's British friend John Isaac Hawkins, offered a solution. His machine had an automatic arm with one pen that moved several others attached to it, making it possible to produce a number of copies at one time. With helpful suggestions from another man of many interests, his friend Thomas Jefferson, Peale was able to perfect the polygraph and use it extensively himself (for which his biographers have been eternally grateful).

Over the years many of Peale's efforts were directed toward promoting good health and long life. In about 1800 he developed a portable steam bath, which he believed was helpful in treating infections, including yellow fever. He also ground lenses for his eyeglasses to improve his vision. But it was the making of false teeth that became an ongoing challenge. Like many people in an era when good dental care was lacking, Peale began to lose his teeth when he was still in his thirties. From that time onward, he had experimented with various materials for false teeth.

As for living to a ripe old age, Peale believed this was possible if people would reform their eating and drinking habits and cultivate serenity of mind. In 1803 he published a long essay offering do's and don'ts for good health. Alcohol and smoking tobacco were to be avoided completely; daily exercise was encouraged. He discussed what to eat (moderate quantities of wholesome food) and how to prepare it (vegetables were to be steamed to preserve their nutritional value). Following his advice, he asserted, would enable people to live two hundred years, which he viewed as "the natural life of man."

In 1810 Peale reached the age of sixty-nine—not even a senior citizen by his reckoning. Nonetheless he announced plans to retire and turn over management of the museum to Rubens. He decided to follow the example of Jefferson, who had retired to his farm at Monticello, Virginia, after leaving the presidency in 1809, and was devoting much of his time to the advancement of science and agriculture. Before long, Peale was writing him the news that he had bought a one-hundred-acre farm near Germantown, just outside Philadelphia. Yet another career had begun for him.

CHAPTER

15

Did anyone really believe Charles Willson Peale when he announced that he was going to retire to his farm "to muse away the remainder of my life"? Far from whiling away the hours in a rocking chair at Belfield, he had an even wider range of activities to keep him busy from dawn to sunset.

The house on the property was badly in need of renovation, and while he was at it Peale added on a studio with skylights and a kitchen with energy-efficient equipment of his own design. With the help of hired labor, crops had to be planted and harvested, farm tools had to be repaired, and there was no end of mechanical inventions to tinker with. Age had not dimmed his energy; increasing deafness was the only sign that he was getting on in years.

In a steady exchange of letters, Peale and Jefferson kept each other informed of new agricultural methods and equipment. At Monticello, the ex-president had invented a moldboard plow, which Peale put into service at Belfield. He also took Jefferson's advice on rotating crops and contour plowing to avoid soil erosion.

Peale's understanding of scientific theories was no match for that of the learned master of Monticello, but his early days as an artisan and his talent for invention enabled him to dream up a number of objects to lighten farm labors. He designed machines for paring apples and planting corn, a more efficient cart for transporting milk to market, and an improved design for a windmill. Only after several costly and disastrous failures did he finally get the windmill to work—the greatest of his follies, he would later admit.

Fruit, vegetables, grain, and milk were the farm's main products. Peale was too fond of animals to raise livestock that would end up being slaughtered. Even the catfish in the pond never made it to the dinner table of the Peale household. In need of a good cash crop, he took a neighbor's advice and planted currants for wine. Because he was totally opposed to drinking alcohol himself, he took this step somewhat reluctantly. The wine of Belfield became the farm's most profitable product, highly praised by Philadelphia wine lovers.

Peale's interest in farming proved to be fairly short-lived. He took greater pleasure in designing and making improvements to farm equipment than he did in the tedious business of growing and marketing crops. Country living also introduced him to a new outlet for his creative energy. Rubens, with his keen interest in botany, began coming out to Belfield to plant trees and shrubs. Soon Peale was lavishing on his garden all the effort and artistic imagination he had given to his museum. In a letter to Jefferson in 1812, he wrote: "Your favorite pursuit, gardening, is also becoming my favorite amusement." It had also become in a sense his outdoor museum.

The beauty of Peale's garden began to attract flocks of people to Belfield. On Sundays the crowds often became so large that the gates had to be closed to keep the flower beds from being crushed. Flowers, shrubs, and exotic trees were only part of the attraction. A fountain and gazebos (small roofed pavilions) decorated the landscape. On the cupola of one gazebo was a bust of George Washington; another was built in a Chinese style. At the end of a walk he erected a tall obelisk. Carefully planned below ground as well as above, the garden had an extensive system of drains so that heavy rain and melting snow could run off.

Although he was absorbed in creating his garden, Peale made time for painting. Most of his work during his long artistic career had been portraits. Now, inspired by the beauty of Belfield, he also did some landscape painting. By 1816 it was evident that he was far less interested in producing crops than he was in making pictures, and much of this renewed interest was due to his son Rembrandt.

The young man had returned from studying art in Paris, where he had learned how to use the encaustic technique, an ancient method of painting that employed wax as a medium. Peale was so impressed by the glowing color effects in Rembrandt's work that he wanted to learn how it was done. The tables were turned, and Rembrandt began to instruct his father, now well into his seventies. As a result of Peale's use of highly glazed colors, his late paintings have a very different look from those done earlier in his career. In the eyes of many critics, he created some of his best work in the final decade of his life.

Peale's "retirement" at Belfield turned out to be very hard on his pocketbook. Not the least of his expenses was the cotton factory he built on the property to provide a business for his sons Linnaeus

View of Garden at Belfield, 1815–1816.

Private Collection. Photograph courtesy of Kennedy Galleries, Inc., New York City.

and Franklin. The children of his second marriage were now approaching adulthood, and he was anxious to see his sons embarked on stable, profitable careers.

Linnaeus's taste for far-flung adventure and thoughts of an army career were particularly upsetting after Peale's own wartime experience. "This does not agree with my Ideas," he wrote to his brother-in-law, "it is a miserable life, and to put oneself in the way of being shot at for $4 a month is a foolish thing at best." Unfortunately the cotton factory eventually failed. Although it produced high-grade cotton, it was unable to compete successfully with less-expensive products.

Peale not only failed to make a profit from the farm but also ended up spending almost all of the money coming to him from the museum just to keep Belfield going. But he had few regrets, as he wrote in his autobiography:

> These amusements cost some money and much time [but] the labors gave health, and happiness is the result of constant employment. His inventions please himself, and they gave pleasure to others. . . . But the economist will say, time, money and labor was misspent. He answers, that happiness is worth millions.

Although management of the museum had been turned over to his son Rubens, Peale was increasingly drawn into solving some of its financial problems. And as he grew older, he became ever more concerned about ensuring a long life for the institution to which he had devoted so many years. When the Philadelphia City Council imposed a sharp increase in rent at the Statehouse in 1816, he began to explore the possibility of moving the museum to either New York City or Washington. New York, he quickly discovered, had more than enough flourishing cultural institutions. Although this was not the case in Washington, his stay in that city from November 1818 to February 1819 dashed all hopes of obtaining federal support. The idea of a national museum met with no more enthusiasm among legislators than it had received during his earlier attempts to win them over.

About the only lasting thing that resulted from his trip to Washington was the large number of portraits he completed and added to his collection at the museum. Among the major political figures he met and painted were President James Monroe, Congressman Henry Clay, and a future president, Andrew Jackson.

In a letter to Jefferson, Peale wrote of his disappointment that the government had failed to act on behalf of his museum: "The time will come when they shall be sorry for having let it slip through their fingers."

Despite his many efforts, Peale never realized his dream of a national museum. Two decades after his death the institution he founded had ceased to exist, and his specimens were sold to such buyers as P. T. Barnum. A number of items were later destroyed by fire. However, the portraits in his Gallery of Great Men have met a kinder fate. The bulk of this collection was bought by the city of Philadelphia when the museum closed. Many of the portraits are now on display in that city as part of the Independence National Historical Park Collection, where they are indeed the legacy Peale had envisioned.

CHAPTER

16

THESE WERE DIFFICULT TIMES FOR THE COUNTRY, AS WELL as for Peale personally. The banking panic of 1819 had led to an extended economic downturn, which caused a severe drop in the museum's earnings. In the midst of these troubles, another yellow-fever epidemic swept the Philadelphia area, and among its victims in 1821 was Peale's wife, Hannah. He also contracted the disease but recovered. Belfield, where they had lived so happily, was leased and eventually sold. Peale returned to Philadelphia and focused on making some decisions about the future of his museum.

With little chance of government support, he decided in 1821 that the best way to ensure a future income from the museum for his children was to incorporate it and issue stock. This would safeguard their rights after his death. As the only stockholder for the time being, Peale appointed a board of five trustees to oversee the museum.

One of their first decisions was to ask Peale to paint a full-length portrait of himself for the museum. In 1822, at the age of eighty-one, he completed *The Artist in His Museum*, which is considered to be his masterpiece. Peale depicted himself raising a curtain so that viewers may see the contents of the museum's Long Room. The portraits of great men and many animal specimens are revealed— all part of his "world in miniature" designed to entertain and edu- cate the public. Behind the curtain, a section of the mastodon can be seen, and on a table are the artist's palette and brushes. Laid aside, they symbolize the fact that Peale has neglected them in order to create his museum.

That same year he once again became its manager. Rubens decided to move to Baltimore and take charge of the museum Rembrandt had established there ten years earlier. With Rembrandt moving to New York to concentrate on his painting career, it was an opportunity for the newly married Rubens to build an indepen- dent future.

In 1824 Peale's memories of revolutionary days were revived when the Marquis de Lafayette paid a formal visit to Philadelphia. The city fathers gave him a hero's welcome, and Peale was under- standably hurt that he was not asked to play an active role in the festivities. Had he not been at Valley Forge with the French noble- man, and also painted his portrait for the Gallery of Great Men? Nothing could keep him from joining the crowd in the Statehouse when Lafayette came to visit the chamber where the Declaration of Independence was signed. Spying his old friend in the crowd, Lafayette rushed over to greet him and then insisted that Peale accompany him to several events.

The following year Raphaelle Peale died at the age of fifty-one. Although he is now acclaimed as a brilliant still-life painter, in his

The Artist in His Museum, 1822.

The Pennsylvania Academy of the Fine Arts, Philadelphia.

Gift of Mrs. Sarah Harrison (The Joseph Harrison, Jr. Collection).

lifetime few people were interested in his work. For many years Peale had sorrowfully witnessed his son's increasing dependence on alcohol. This no doubt contributed to his death, but it is now considered quite likely that his work at the museum preserving specimens led to arsenic and mercury poisoning of his system. What is difficult to believe is that Peale was to blame for his son's death, a theory recently advanced that has caused scholarly controversy.

According to this theory, Peale must have known the cause of Raphaelle's illness and could have supplied an antidote to relieve his suffering but failed to act out of jealousy over his son's talent. An entirely different picture emerges in a reading of Peale's many letters to Raphaelle in which he expresses loving concern and appreciation of his still-life paintings. Perhaps even more convincing were Peale's efforts over the years to provide Raphaelle with a stable income.

It is apparent, however, that Peale never really understood his eldest son. Much as he admired Raphaelle's ability as a still-life painter, Peale believed that portrait painting was a higher type of art and urged his son to follow this path. At the same time, Peale did not hide his opinion that Raphaelle's portraits were mediocre. Economically dependent on his father all his life, Raphaelle never managed to escape Peale's dominating presence.

Living in the shadow of a dynamo like Charles Willson Peale was particularly difficult for Raphaelle, but it could not have been easy for his other sons as well. He was a hard act to follow, yet many of them chose careers in art or the sciences. As Peale's many letters to all of them indicate, he was deeply concerned about their welfare, although he probably offered more advice and sermons than they wanted to read. But his attentions stemmed from an abiding devotion to his family.

Peale was an active letter writer all his life, but it was not until he was well into his eighties that he decided to write his autobiography. Fortunately there were copies of his letters and diaries to jog his memory of bygone days. It was time, he said, to give an honest accounting of his life. This made some of the Peale offspring a bit uneasy. Having attained a certain position in society (thanks largely to their father's accomplishments), they didn't want to be embarrassed by anything the unpredictable old gentleman might reveal. Peale usually visited with his daughter Sophy in the evening, reading to her the latest installment of his memoirs, and she did her best to censor things of which she disapproved.

Peale was still capable of coming up with a venture that some of his children felt was undignified for him. After many years of experimenting with one material or another for false teeth, he had begun working with porcelain. By 1826 he had succeeded in producing a set of teeth that had a natural appearance and also fitted well. He was so delighted with the results that he decided to manufacture them. To the horror of the younger Peales, he announced his new venture in a Philadelphia newspaper in May 1826. None of them had any complaints about his making false teeth for himself or members of the family, but going into the business struck them as socially unacceptable. It was not a booming success, as the teeth cost $150—a good sum in those days. Nonetheless, Peale's name has gone down in the annals of dentistry for his work.

The family uproar over this venture, as well as quarrels among his children over money matters, upset the domestic harmony that had always been important to Peale. He had been living with Titian Ramsay II and his wife, but longed to marry again. By this time he had concluded that reaching the age of two hundred was probably too much to expect but thought that one hundred was surely possible. In that case, at the age of eighty-six, there was still time for a happy marriage.

An acquaintance recommended an elderly lady who taught at a school for the deaf in New York. Given his own hearing problems, Peale thought that Mary Stansbury seemed like a good prospect. Ever the fast worker, even at his advanced age, he made a trip to New York to meet her. Within a few days he proposed, also offering to give the startled woman lessons in making false teeth. Neither offer was accepted.

The disappointed suitor headed back to Philadelphia by boat. In stormy weather it ran aground almost a mile before the landing. Peale had to trudge a long distance carrying a heavy trunk and other belongings. Exhausted by the effort, the old man could barely make his way. At home he began to suffer sharp pains and realized he had strained his heart. As the weeks passed, his condition grew steadily worse. He tried to rouse himself to help plan for the museum's move to larger quarters, but he was too weak. Death came on February 22, 1827.

On the day of his funeral, a long line of carriages slowly wended its way to St. Peter's churchyard, not far from the house on Lombard Street where his first gallery had been opened. Just as Peale had reached out in so many different directions over the course of his eighty-six years, people from all walks of life came to pay their respects. Artists, his fellow members of the American Philosophical Society, old veterans of the Revolution, and politicians who recalled the stormy days of the "Furious Whigs" were among the throng.

There are many who have said that Charles Willson Peale should have concentrated on his artistic and scientific endeavors instead of spending so much time on other things. He acknowledged the fact that he had "strayed a thousand ways," but was quick to add that this had contributed to his happiness. Yet all his pursuits were unified by a striving toward human progress that reflected the spirit of the age in which he lived, and to which he contributed so much.

SELECTED BIBLIOGRAPHY

Cikovsky, Jr., Nicolai, et al. *Raphaelle Peale Still-Lifes*. Washington, D.C.: National Gallery of Art, 1988.

Elam, Charles H., ed. *The Peale Family: Three Generations of American Artists*. Detriot: Detroit Institute of Arts and Wayne State University Press, 1967.

Flexner, James Thomas. *America's Old Masters: First Artists of the New World*. New York: Viking Press, 1939.

Four Generations of Commissions: The Peale Collection of the Maryland Historical Society. Baltimore: Maryland Historical Society, 1975.

Miller, Lillian B., ed. *The Selected Papers of Charles Willson Peale and His Family*. 4 vols. New Haven: Yale University Press, 1983–1995. (Vols. 5 to 7 forthcoming. Vol 5 will contain Peale's autobiography.)

These volumes draw on the extensive holdings of Peale manuscripts in the library of the American Philosophical Society, and others from the Historical Society of Pennsylvania and other sources.

Miller, Lillian B., and David C. Ward, eds. *New Perspectives on Charles Willson Peale*. Pittsburgh: University of Pittsburgh Press, 1991.

Miller, Lillian B. *In Pursuit of Fame: Rembrandt Peale, 1778–1860.* Seattle and Washington, D.C.: National Portrait Gallery, Smithsonian Institution, and University of Washington Press, 1992.

Peale, Charles Willson. "The Life of Charles Willson Peale," unpublished autobiography, in *The Papers of Charles Willson Peale and His Family: A Microfiche Edition.* Lillian B. Miller, ed. Millwood, N.Y.: Kraus Thomson Publishers, 1980.

Richardson, E.P., Brooke Hindle, and Lillian B. Miller, eds. *Charles Willson Peale and His World.* New York: Harry N. Abrams, 1982.

Sellers, Charles Coleman. *Charles Willson Peale.* New York: Charles Scribner's Sons, 1969.

————. *Mr. Peale's Museum: Charles Willson Peale and the First Popular Museum of Natural Science and Art.* New York: Norton, 1980.

Ward, David C., and Sidney Hart. "Subversion and Illusion in the Life and Art of Raphaelle Peale." In *American Art* (Summer/Fall 1994): 97–121. This article contains an interesting discussion of Charles Willson Peale's views on bringing up children and also details his troubled relationship with his son Raphaelle.

INDEX